Strengthen What Remains Combo Set

A Novella and Novelette in the Strengthen What Remains series

By Kyle Pratt

CAMDEN CASCADE
PUBLISHING

Strengthen What Remains Combo Set
By Kyle Pratt

Copyright © 2016 Kyle Pratt
ISBN: 978-0-9969412-9-7
First Edition – October 2016
All Rights Reserved
Editor: Barbara Blakey
Cover Design: Micah Hansen
Interior Design: Amit Dey

Sign up for my no-spam monthly newsletter and get a free ebook.
Details are at the end of the novel.

Table of Contents

Nightmare in Slow Motion

This is a novelette in the Strengthen What Remains *series. The characters and setting of this 13,000 word story are from* Through Many Fires, A Time to Endure *and* Braving the Storms. *Several readers of those books asked me for more details about what happened to Caden's older brother, Peter. This is Peter's story.*

From the top floor of the abandoned hospital, Renton police officer Peter Westmore stared across a vast expanse of the southern Seattle metro area. After the evacuation of Renton he had been assigned to general evacuation duty.

Swirling black smoke climbed into the cold February wind from a fire a block away. Looters had started the blaze earlier in the morning and that had probably cut power to the hospital, but the terrorists were the more ominous threat. Out there, somewhere, they had a nuclear bomb, and threatened to detonate it at any moment.

The fear churning through him had brought back a childhood nightmare. Satan, with huge horns, a wicked grin, and whip-like tail pursued him. As hard as he tried to run, he barely moved. Every time he looked over his shoulder the wicked demon drew closer. In that awful dream Peter had struggled with all the might of his young legs to get away, but Satan leapt upon him.

Now, years later, he stood on the top floor of the hospital and felt that urge to flee grow like a storm in his gut. Once again he tried to call his wife. The phone showed a good signal. He tapped "Sue" on his contact list, but it didn't connect.

He pressed transmit on his radio. "Leon, the top floor is clear."

"Roger. I'll meet you on the roof."

As Peter ran from the room, the lights flickered and died. He hoped this didn't mean a new problem, but that the generator had merely run out of gas.

Using his flashlight, Peter took the dark steps two at a time.

On the roof a doctor and two nurses loaded the last three patients into the waiting copter.

Although Peter wanted desperately to leave and head south, out of the range of the nuclear bomb, he waited by the stairwell door for his partner of nearly three years to climb to the roof.

An American flag fluttered nearby. The wind blew from the west. He looked north toward Seattle and thought of Sue. Again he tried to contact her on the phone. Again he failed.

The last nurse had just climbed aboard when Leon dashed from the stairwell. Together they ran to the helicopter.

The pilot shouted over the roar of the blades. "I'm sorry, I'm already overweight."

Anger, mixed with fear, rose within Peter. Again, just like in his dream, he wanted to flee, but couldn't.

The pilot pushed the throttle forward producing a frigid whirlwind.

Peter and Leon stumbled back as the helo rose into a cloudy gray sky, and then turned toward the south and safety.

"Was that the last helicopter?" Peter asked as the sound of the blades died in the distance.

"I think so." Leon walked to the parapet.

Peter joined him. Below sirens wailed, horns honked, and people shouted and screamed in an endless slow-motion struggle south.

"We are so screwed." Leon shook his head.

"Our patrol car is still in the parking lot."

"Do you really think we can get to safety in a car?" Leon looked down at the vehicles below. "It doesn't have much gas."

"I need to get home to my wife any way I can, and right now the squad car is the best option."

"I thought you phoned your dad and asked him to take Sue to the family farm."

Peter sighed. "I did, but we got cut off before Dad replied. I'm not sure he heard me ask."

Leon nodded. "Okay, let's go."

Peter hurried from the roof with Leon right behind. Racing down one dark flight of stairs after another it seemed they would never reach the first floor and the squad car.

When they did burst into the lobby daylight, the stillness and silence stunned Peter. Glancing over his shoulder for any oncoming devils, he turned and rushed toward the exit. Suddenly a car horn broke the silence of the empty building.

Leon shook his head. "If it were night, this would be really creepy."

"It's still creepy." Peter pointed down an empty corridor. "This way."

As they hurried, the blaring horn grew louder.

The two officers pulled open a sliding door and rushed out.

In the driver's seat of a nearby car, a woman rocked back and forth as she pounded the steering wheel.

Peter jogged over to the vehicle just outside of the emergency room.

The young woman grimaced, leaned back hard against the seat, and beat on the horn.

"Are you okay?" The pained look on her face told him she wasn't. She wore a loose coat, but appeared to have a large belly. *I'll practice my investigative skills. Young woman, large belly, pain, at a hospital entrance. You're in labor.* But, still he asked, "What's wrong?"

"Contractions."

Peter bit his lip. This was not a good time to be having a baby. "How can I help?" He heard footsteps and glanced over his shoulder. Leon approached.

Her eyes darted between Peter and his partner. Tension seemed to flow from her. She breathed deeply. "Can you help me into the hospital?"

Leon shook his head.

"It's deserted," Peter frowned. "We were about to leave."

Her mouth dropped. "Deserted?" Tears flowed.

"Has your water broken?" Peter asked.

Her teeth gritted, she nodded.

"How far apart are the contractions?" Leon asked.

"About five minutes."

Peter's thoughts turned to his own pregnant wife. He prayed for Sue's safety and vowed to return to her as soon as possible. "Leon, get the squad car."

His partner sprinted away.

"Let me help you out." Before she pulled out the key, Peter glanced at her gas gauge. Inwardly he sighed. Empty. "We'll take you to North Hillcrest Community Hospital. It's farther south, and last I heard, still open."

"Still open?" She grimaced. "It could be closed too?"

"I'm sure it's still in operation. Peter spoke with more confidence than he held. "Is this your first child?"

She nodded, and slid her feet to the pavement.

"Hold my arm." He eased her from the car. "What's your name?"

"Leslie." She stood with a moan. "My husband's in the army. They deployed his unit after the D. C. blast. I don't even know where he is." Tears rolled down her cheeks.

Leon pulled up in the squad car as a cold drizzle filled the air. Together the two men helped Leslie into the back seat.

Peter drove away from the empty hospital and raced down several nearly deserted side streets. The stillness amid the chaos made the day all the more foreboding, but soon they reached the gridlocked line of traffic headed to the freeway. Peter tried to console himself with the fact that they were at least pointed south, but now he grew even more certain his childhood nightmare had become real. The three of them were caught in a sea of people that wanted to speed away from Seattle, but at best, crawled at an agonizingly slow pace.

The metro region had awoken to news that terrorists had a nuclear bomb in Seattle. The exodus that had ebbed and flowed from the urban areas for nearly a week turned into a panicked gridlock. Peter looked at the speedometer and knew he could walk faster. Some people did walk along the edge of the freeway. Others ran. They inched past a car with doors ajar, but no one inside. How many of those fleeing on foot had abandoned their cars and added to the traffic problems of others?

A stream of police calls crackled across the radio. Like the roads, every channel seemed filled with urgent messages and few answers.

After repeated attempts, Leon reported their position, their passenger, and destination. "However, we are currently stuck in gridlocked traffic and will be unable to respond to calls."

"Roger. Keep heading south. You might be far enough away if the blast comes."

But they weren't heading anywhere. Traffic had halted. Peter glanced at the gas gauge. Less than a quarter of a tank remained. He looked in the rearview mirror at their passenger. Leslie's grimace revealed her pain.

The maniacs had proven in Washington D. C., ten days ago, that they were willing to detonate their weapons and die for their cause. The horror had been repeated in Los Angeles, Atlanta and other cities. Now he lived the nightmare.

He looked again in the mirror. With each glance he expected to see a demonic mushroom cloud, but this time he saw only gray sky.

He retrieved his cell phone and tried to call Sue.

Only silence met his ear.

Peter shoved the useless device back into his pocket, and eased the police cruiser forward a few inches.

People ran and jogged along both sides of the highway. The old and those with children trotted or walked. They crept past more abandoned vehicles as the squad car gas gauge dipped toward empty.

He pressed the brake and stopped inches from the bumper of the car in front.

Minutes passed and they moved forward a few yards. People now moved among the vehicles as if through a parking lot.

He glanced again in the mirror. No mushroom cloud, just a very pregnant shifting and moaning woman in the back seat.

"I'm convinced that there are three types of people in the world," Leon said.

"What?" Peter raised an eyebrow and glanced at his partner.

"Yeah, there are three types."

"Okay…good, bad and what?"

Leon shook his head. "Those who panic early and those who panic late."

"You said, there were three types of people. What's the third?"

"Those, like us, who never panic."

Since they were barely moving, Peter took a long look at Leon. "The gates of hell are about to open behind us, we're barely moving and you're not scared?"

"Being scared is normal. Panic is…" He looked at the endless mass of cars and people crowding down the broad highway. "Panic is useless. I don't mind saying all this scares me, the other cities being nuked, the FBI finding a terror cell in Seattle, the evacuation order—"

Leslie released a loud groan.

Leon turned to her. "Your baby will be fine. How are you doing?

Peter again called his wife. He put the phone to his ear, but heard nothing from it. He shoved it in a pocket and turned so he could see both Leon and Leslie. "If we don't want to deliver a baby on the freeway, we better come up with a plan to get her to a hospital."

Leon snapped his fingers. "I have an idea. I'll drive for a while." He exited the car and walked around the front.

"That's your plan?" Peter looked south down the line of cars. "It's more like parking."

"You go be a traffic cop and get us to that off-ramp there." Leon pointed south. "The side streets are moving better than the freeway."

Peter stepped out.

Leon slid into the driver's seat and turned on the light bar.

Peter leaned against the door. "You didn't want to drive. You just wanted to play with the lights."

His partner smiled. "I thought I handled that rather smoothly."

"Arghhhhhhh," came from Leslie.

Peter stood in the middle of the freeway directing traffic. A car rolled toward the spot Peter wanted for the squad car. He stepped in front of it, wagging his finger, and mouthing, "No, no, no."

The driver, a man in his forties, flushed red, but stopped.

Leon drove into the lane and Peter walked over to the next. After nearly a half hour of traffic direction and maneuvering, the squad car arrived at the exit.

Peter walked ahead of their vehicle, up the off ramp, asking drivers to pull over as far to the right as they could. This created a lane for Leon to drive the car ahead. Farther south on the freeway shots rang out. He stared in that direction for a moment, but resisted the urge to investigate. Looking toward Leon, he waved. "Follow me."

"Hey!" A man with a scruffy beard and wearing a worn brown jacket shouted, "I need to talk to you."

The man hurried toward him, Peter felt uneasy. The coat could easily conceal a weapon. As he neared, Peter held his hand up in a stop motion. "That's close enough." His hand rested on his Glock.

The man gritted his teeth. "I'm out of gas."

"What do you want us to do?" Peter stepped back closer to the cruiser.

"Ah…well…You've got gas. Give me some. I don't need much."

Peter shook his head. "You and tens of thousands of others need gas, a spare tire, radiator fluid—and a dozen other things. Sorry, we're on our way to the hospital." He pointed down the street. "I'm not sure we have enough to get there. Perhaps you should—"

"If the terrorists set off that bomb now … me, my family, we'll die."

Peter looked around at the sea of cars and people. "If a nuclear bomb goes off anytime soon, all of us will die."

"I have a Rolex. You could have it for a few gallons of gas."

Peter eyed the man hard. How had this man in worn clothes gotten an expensive watch? He shook his head. "I don't need it."

The man wilted at Peter's words.

Despite the attempted bribery, Peter remained empathic, but there was little he could do. "Take your family to the hospital. They have a shelter."

The man turned and ran back toward the freeway.

Leon rolled down the window. "The gas gauge is on the 'E,' and Leslie is running out of time. That is, unless you want to play doctor."

A moan boomed from the backseat.

Peter nodded, walked ahead, and continued to clear a lane for the squad car. As he did, he thought about Sue. She was far enough south that the blast and radiation probably wouldn't reach her, but in the growing panic he wondered what other insanities might occur. His little brother, Caden, lived in Washington, D. C., and had probably died the night of that first blast. Peter hoped his death came quickly.

The roar of engines caused Peter to look back toward the freeway. Several motorcycles weaved around the unmoving vehicles. Such maneuvers were illegal in Washington State, but the riders would probably live. He wasn't so sure about everyone else.

A woman in a blue Lexus SUV rolled down her window. "Can you get this traffic moving?"

"Not if my life depended upon it," Peter replied. *And it just might.*

"What are we supposed to do?" she asked.

"We're headed to the hospital. If you're going that way, try to follow."

The roads remained congested as they inched away from the freeway, but traffic crawled forward at a more consistent pace. Leon maneuvered the squad car forward along the street, through parking lots and down sidewalks. A line of vehicles formed behind them as other drivers realized the squad car was moving, albeit slowly, south.

Minutes later Peter jogged down a side street, gesturing and yelling for vehicles to move to the side so the squad car could pass. Even on cold wet days like this one he liked to run. It gave him time to think, and now those thoughts were of Sue, pregnant and alone. *Please God, let her be okay. I'm coming.*

Even in rush-hour traffic his commute took less than an hour, but with the traffic today, it would take much longer. He looked back at the squad car. Each step brought him closer to Sue, but his southward jog was gut-wrenchingly slow.

He pointed for a van to pull to the side of the road.

As they neared the hospital, the traffic grew heavier until they were again jammed in a line of motionless vehicles.

Peter trotted back to the side of the patrol car. "How is Leslie doing?"

The engine sputtered and died.

A groan issued from the backseat.

"Oh, she could be better." Leon tried to restart the vehicle several times. "We're out of gas." He looked down the line of motionless cars. "You know this area better than I do; how close are we to the hospital?"

"About a half mile … no less." Peter pointed to a tall building. "It's just beyond that."

Leon sighed. "Let's push the squad car to the side of the road and help Leslie to the hospital."

With the car against the curb, Leon grasped the mic and tried to report their situation and position. "I can't get through," he said after several attempts.

"Come on, help me with Leslie." Peter opened the backdoor. "We'll get her to the hospital and maybe they have a way to contact our department." He stood on one side of Leslie, and Leon on the other, as they walked from the useless vehicle.

"Why are they all jammed onto this road?" Peter waved his arm at the line of cars.

"What better place to be, if you can't get away, than at a hospital?"

As they walked by, Peter looked at the people in the cars. Age made no difference; they were all frightened. Some cried.

"Arghhhhhhh." The muscles in Leslie's neck stood tense. Her brow furrowed as she stopped and panted. "It's not going to be long now." After a moment, she stumbled forward.

Leon shifted her weight onto him. "Let's hurry." He stepped forward.

A car inched across their path.

Peter waved for it to stop.

The three hurried across the street.

As they passed the tall building Peter had indicated, the modern steel and glass five-story hospital came into view. A helicopter lifted off from the building roof.

Peter and Leon carried her down the street and across the jammed parking lot as another chopper approached.

"They're evacuating the hospital." Leon shook his head as he pointed to the helo.

"No!" Leslie cast him an angry look. "Not before I get there."

"Don't worry." Peter gestured toward approaching helicopters. "If the choppers are still coming, doctors are still there."

Straining and groaning, Leslie hung on as the three hurried the last hundred yards to the hospital.

A crush of people bumped and jostled Peter as they moved across the emergency room. Doctors and nurses rushed through with gurneys and wheelchairs. It wasn't chaos, but it wasn't far from it.

Peter stepped in front of a nurse. "This woman is in labor."

The nurse pointed. "Check in at the admissions desk."

He stood just over six feet tall, but through the mass of people Peter couldn't see a counter. When he looked back the nurse had disappeared into the multitude.

The three weaved, pushed, and apologized their way across the lobby to a kiosk and one beleaguered admissions clerk.

Leaning against the counter, Peter gestured with one hand. "This woman—"

The clerk held a finger up to Peter, clutched a phone receiver in her other hand and spoke to an orderly nearby. "Take the man with gunshot wounds to room five. The lady with the compound fracture goes to seven."

A young man rolled an empty gurney to the counter and spoke to the clerk. "Where do you want this?"

The clerk, now speaking on the phone, didn't seem to hear.

In his most official voice, Peter said, "Take this woman to maternity—stat!"

Peter and Leon helped Leslie onto the gurney.

"Thank you." Worry seemed to ebb from her as the young man wheeled her away.

Peter waved as she disappeared into the crowd. He felt a weight of responsibility lift. Now, he and Leon could focus on their own journey to safety. With a tilt of the head, he indicated a nearby side exit. "Let's get out of here."

Stepping out a door, Peter spotted a state patrol mobile command center. "We should check in. Maybe they have communications with our department."

As they jogged across the parking lot, Leon pointed to a police lieutenant standing with other patrol officers near the command center. They changed direction and headed directly toward the officers.

The lieutenant wiped his forehead. "What do you guys need?"

Leon slowed to a walk. "We can't communicate with our department, so we thought we'd check in here."

He shook his head. "The command center is heading south, pronto."

Worry about Peter's own family churned constantly in his gut, but the mention of south brought the anxiety to the forefront of his mind. Hopefully, his wife and unborn son were safe on the family farm, but they might be less than thirty-five miles from where he stood, at their suburban home. He wanted to be with them. He wanted, needed, to run to her. Instead, he nodded. "Can you spare some gasoline?"

"Or give us a ride," Leon added.

"No to both. Sorry. We're full up with others who need a ride and we're short on gas, but...." He opened the trunk of a nearby patrol car and pulled out an orange case and a five gallon gas can. "Siphon the gas from the car of any doctor. They won't need the fuel. They're being evacuated by air to Madigan Army Medical Center, along with the patients."

"Thanks." Peter took the kit from the lieutenant.

The two hurried toward the reserved section of the parking lot, Leon looked up at a helicopter as it lifted from the roof and sped south. He laughed.

Peter shook his head. "What could be funny right now?"

"It occurred to me that Leslie will probably reach safety long before we do."

"That's funny?"

Leon shrugged. "In a macabre, ironic, sort of way ... sure."

Again, Peter thought of Sue. "Come on, let's get moving." He picked out a car and ran to it ahead of Leon.

Peter already had gas flowing into the can when Leon caught up.

The can was nearly full when the lieutenant pulled alongside them in a squad car packed with other officers. "The navy has the terrorists surrounded on a fishing boat just off of West Seattle. Military, Homeland Security and police are moving in. They're trying to talk them into surrendering." He shook his head. "If the other attacks are any indication, these jihadists are intent on dying and taking a lot of people with them. It won't be long now."

Peter nodded and looked north. "Thanks." He grabbed the gas can and dashed across the parking lot.

"Wait for me," Leon yelled.

Peter didn't answer as he ran back toward the squad car.

On a normal day this amount of traffic would have been considered heavy but, here the vehicles at least moved, albeit slowly, unlike the freeway and many other streets. Peter looked forward to heading south again. He dashed around the creeping vehicles to reach the squad car. Staring north he poured the gas into the tank. The normally noxious fumes now smelled like hope as they chugged reluctantly from the can into the tank.

Leon ran up, flew into the car, and started it.

Peter tossed the empty can and siphon kit in the trunk, ran to the passenger side and jumped in as Leon popped the car into gear.

Tires squealed.

Leon slid and bumped his way into the southern flow of traffic.

Again, Peter tried to phone Sue, but heard nothing. A half-mile farther along the road, he glimpsed the freeway. It reminded him of a logjam on a river. Still, Peter remained hopeful that in a couple of hours he would be home. Even the cold drizzling rain had stopped.

Barely three miles south of the hospital, a high-pitched squeal reverberated from the radio.

The car sputtered and died.

Leon spun around in his seat.

Slumping forward, Peter shouted, "Cover your eyes!"

In the side mirror Peter glimpsed a helicopter as it fell from the sky, crashed on a nearby apartment building, and burst into a ball of flame. He pressed his eyes closed and threw his arms over them. Even so, red light shined through. "Too close! We're still too close!"

Screams echoed in his ears.

Several moments later, when the light faded, he opened his eyes.

A boiling mushroom cloud grew in the north. Lightning lit the sky. The gates of hell had been thrown open and every demon Peter ever imagined danced in the fire-laced storm.

The top of a nearby apartment building burned like a torch where the helicopter had crashed.

Typhoon-like gusts shook the car and peppered it with stones and debris. A myriad of cracks spread out across the rear window.

"No! No!" Leon slammed his fist on the steering wheel and dash.

"Don't panic now," Peter rested a hand on his shoulder. "The pulse from the blast burned out the car's electronics."

Leon fumbled with the keys. Then he turned to Peter with terror-filled eyes. "I can't see."

"It's flash blindness. In a few hours your vision will … should get better." Peter glanced at the ever growing cloud. "Right now we need to find shelter."

Thunder boomed across the sky.

Peter shook his partner with one hand and opened the car door with the other. "We've got to go! I'll lead you." The storm seized the door and yanked it from Peter's hand. He stepped into the tempest.

The wind carried the sound of screams, prayers, and cries for help.

Peter struggled to keep his footing as the growing throng of people buffeted and pushed against him. Dust spun in the air. He knew this area, but in the windstorm landmarks were hard to see. Voices shouted out of the wind.

Leon planted both hands on the squad car. "Where do we go?"

A panicked hoard emerged from the dust storm. Like a swarm of locusts they rushed southward threatening to destroy all that they encountered.

Peter clutched Leon's hand and placed it on his belt. "Grab ahold. Don't let go!"

The veneer of orderly conduct stripped away as screams, from soprano to tenor, filled the air. Ten yards away a little girl fell. A woman screamed as others trampled the child. Still more tripped over the bloody body and were crushed by the throng. No one stopped.

Peter stepped into the flow of people.

Leon tugged on his belt.

Peter veered toward the edge like a swimmer exiting a riptide. "Still with me?"

"Still here!" Leon shouted.

Peter struggled to keep pace with the mob, and not be flung to the ground by it, as he angled out of the flow. A gray snow fell from the sky. It seemed too soon for fallout to pour down, but he couldn't be sure. How much had he inhaled? He tried not to breathe. To survive they needed to get off the street.

The day grew ever darker as dust blotted every hint of the sun's disk.

Ahead Peter spotted the vague outline of a stone bank building, built nearly a hundred years earlier. He called over his shoulder. "Hold tight."

Leon tugged on the belt. "I am!"

Seconds later Peter felt a sharp tug on his belt. "Hang on. We're almost there."

He heard Leon's voice, but didn't catch the words.

It took nearly a minute to bump and push across the panicked flow of humanity and emerge near the entrance of the bank. He turned to Leon, but he stood alone. He called to his partner, as panic rose within him. He shouted, but his voice was absorbed in the countless voices carried on the wind around him. Peter scanned the crowd, but didn't see Leon. Somewhere in the mass of frightened people his blind partner struggled to survive.

An old woman with blank eyes, slammed into Peter, and nearly knocked him down.

He reached for her.

Their hands touched.

Others pushed and bumped into her.

She spun around and stumbled along with the flow of the frightened mob.

As Peter watched, she disappeared from view. *Like Leon?* A noise behind him caught his attention. A cluster of people gathered under the portico of the old stone bank building. The group probably gathered there because of the cover, but such structures often had basements and fallout shelters. With one last look for Leon, he jogged toward them, others joined the huddled throng of people.

Tan and gray dust covered everything like light snow. Several men banged on the glass that formed most of the door.

"Stand back," Peter said with greater calm than he felt. He pulled his weapon from the holster and fired a shot that shattered the glass.

An older man, with thinning gray-haired man and wearing a sports jacket, kicked out most of the remaining shards.

A middle-aged man in a three-piece business suit, hurried through, cutting himself on one hand as he did.

The older man took off his jacket and used it to break out more of the glass. "Be careful," he said with a British accent. Then he helped several women and children into the building.

Peter counted seventeen people pass through the door. Then all that remained were him and the British gentleman. Peter gestured for him to enter.

With a nod he did.

Peter looked over his shoulder for Leon and then took a black marker from his pocket and on the unbroken glass pane of the adjoining door wrote, "19 survivors inside." He followed the others into the dark bank building.

When he stepped inside the man with the British accent pointed to the notice of survivors. "Is that for searchers?"

Peter nodded.

"I hope they see it."

The group gathered in the middle of the lobby. Peter dusted off his clothes and ran fingers through his short dark hair. The sports jacket man did the same, followed by several women as the brushing action moved through the group. Some cried.

Peter wondered how much radioactive fallout they were brushing off—and how much remained on them. Without a word to the wretched group, he went in search of the basement.

That morning he awoke as a police officer, sworn to uphold the law. He had assisted with the evacuation of one hospital and brought Leslie safely to another. Since then he had stolen gasoline and broke into a building. He felt no guilt, but those events reminded him how quickly, and drastically, life had changed.

Peter spotted a faded fallout shelter sign and jogged toward it.

"Where are you going?" the man in a business suit asked.

"To find that shelter." Peter pointed to the sign.

The man laughed. "Those haven't been used since the cold war."

The British man shook his head. "But it would still be there."

"Would we be safe inside?" a woman asked.

"Safer than outside and safer than here." Peter gestured toward several large windows. "Gamma radiation flows right through those."

The man in the three-piece suit wrapped his cut hand in paper towels. "How come you know so much?"

"My dad's a prepper," Peter said walking away.

"A what?"

"Someone who's prepared," he said over his shoulder. Peter continued on following the faded fallout signs to a stone stairway at the back of the building.

Others followed.

Out of habit he flipped a nearby light switch and then grumbled when no illumination appeared. He grasped his flashlight and proceeded down the stairs. Others used their cellphones as lights, but Peter wanted to save the battery.

Deep shadows and stale air greeted him as he descended the steps. From the landing at the bottom he could see eight doors, four on each side. The nearest had a sign, "Storeroom 1," and an expensive keypad lock. The next door, "Storeroom 2," used a deadbolt. Peter considered kicking the doors open or using his pistol, but decided to check each before resorting to such measures. The next two doors were label as storerooms and locked.

The fifth door still had the "Men's Room" sign on it and opened to a small restroom with antique plumbing. The next led to the women's room.

The seventh door was simply labeled "Janitor" and stood unlocked.

Peter stepped into a musty, windowless supply room. He coughed on the stale air, but knew it wouldn't kill him, like the fallout-laced air outside. He nodded at the thought that this might have been the original fallout shelter. If not, it would still provide the protection they needed. Metal shelves, stacked with cleaning supplies, lined both sides of the gray room. At the rear were buffers, brooms and a deep sink. Peter turned the hot water valve.

Only gurgling came forth.

The cold water faucet produced a slow drip. He turned it off. "We need to gather all the water and supplies we can find." Peter pointed to a young man and woman holding tightly to each other. "You two find the breakroom and bring all the water and food here. Water is more important than food, so do that first."

They nodded and left.

"We'll need to remove the mops, buckets and other cleaning supplies. Then take the shelves out, to make enough room for all nineteen of us.

The British accent gentleman gripped a buffer.

"My name is Peter." He touched the man's arm.

"Mine is Anthony." He said with a nod of the head.

"Are you from England?" Peter asked.

"Yes, many years ago."

The two shook hands.

Several women grabbed cleaning supplies from a shelf and walked away.

Most of the others stood in the hall with blank expressions.

Holding an armful of cleaning supplies, Peter shook his head at the frightened cluster. "I know we've been through a lot today, but I'm going to need your help preparing the room if we're going to live." Peter dropped the articles in the hall and turned to gather more.

Several others followed him into the room.

The only light in the hallway shined down from upstairs. The storeroom stood around the corner, but near enough to the steps to receive some light. Did the pale glow bring gamma radiation? His father would have known. Instead of thinking he had a weird dad, he now wished he had paid more attention. He set the flashlight high on a shelf where it provided additional, albeit limited, light for the room.

"Where do you want all this cleaning stuff?" a young man with long brown hair asked.

"Just dump it outside. We don't need to be neat."

As Peter turned to leave, with hands full, the man in the three-piece suit stood in the doorway. "That's your plan? Clear out the room? Then what? Die in there?"

"No." Peter shook his head. "If we can find enough water, I plan to survive in there until searchers find us or most of the fallout clears. Now, get out of my way."

"How long will that take?" three-piece suit grumbled, but stood aside.

Since he had no idea, Peter didn't answer.

By the time the couple returned with a half-filled water cooler jug much of the cleaning gear had been emptied from the room.

"The pipes just gurgle." The young man said. "No water comes out."

Peter hadn't expected the upstairs faucets to work, but they would need more water both for drinking and washing. He forced a smile. "We can get some water from there." He pointed to the deep sink. "You did good. Go, see—"

"Good?" Three-piece suit grabbed the jug. "Have you counted? There are nineteen people in this building. How long do you think this water will last us?"

"What's your name?" Peter asked politely.

"Why?"

So, I know who the jerk in the group is. So, I don't have to refer to you as, Pain in my Butt. "Oh, it just makes conversation easier. My name is Peter."

"Yeah, I heard you and Anthony get acquainted. Well, mine is Blaine, Blaine Harrison."

"Nice to meet you, Blaine," Peter said without a hint of sarcasm. "Do you know how to find more water or do you have a better plan?"

Blaine hesitated. "Well, no, not right now, but this won't do."

Anger flared within Peter. Blaine criticized his ideas without bothering to figure out something better. Peter clenched his fist and considered using it across the man's face, but instead he took a deep breath. "Perhaps we should continue what we're doing until a better plan comes along."

Blaine thrust the water bottle into Peter's arms, grunted, and walked away.

Peter turned back to the couple that found the jug of water. "Collect any water that comes from the deep sink. Then go find any food that is in the building. Break into snack machines or whatever else you have to do."

As he set the bottle in the corner of the storeroom Peter noticed a woman grab a crowbar from a shelf. "Could I have that?" With it, he hurried to the first storeroom. With several grunts and pushes he pried it open and stepped in. Stacked to the ceiling were office supplies, furniture and old computer equipment. With a sigh he moved to the next where he discovered old paper files. The third room, labeled "Utility," contained what he had hoped to find, the water heater. "Yes!"

Anthony stood in the doorway with a confused look. "What's got you excited?"

Peter leaned on the tank. "Fifty gallons of water. We need a hose and some empty water cooler bottles or buckets."

Anthony smiled. "I'll find them."

Stepping from the room Peter called out. "I need everyone over here." As they gathered, he continued. "When Anthony returns we need to use some of this water to wash our skin and hair."

"What?." Blaine frowned. "That's most of our water and you want to bathe with it?"

"Just some. So we can get the radioactive fallout off our hair and skin."

Blaine looked at his still dusty sleeve, and then cast a disgruntled look at Peter, but within minutes the others were draining the water.

"Save this water." Peter said as he gazed at the group. "We'll use it to flush the toilets."

The women filled a couple of buckets and then moved to the storeroom to use the deep sink. The men remained where they were.

Minutes later a woman returned with wet hair and two empty buckets.

"Limit your use of water." Peter tapped the tank. "What we don't wash with we'll be drinking."

Later, as they gathered in the storeroom, Anthony looked over the supplies. "We don't have much food."

Peter nodded. "That's true." In the corner were two water cooler jugs and a small mound of candy bars, potato chips and cookies. They also had whatever remained in the heater. "If we ration the supplies I think we can survive a week. Water will be the limiting factor. When that runs out we'll have three to five days."

Anthony looked grim. "I'll set up a rationing system."

Peter smiled. "Thanks." He pulled his phone out, intending to call Sue, but the device wouldn't turn on. He sighed and shoved it into a pocket.

The next few days blurred together. The normal dim light of the storeroom gave way to darkness, and then returned to twilight and more darkness. Had they been there two or three days? Peter pressed the stem of his watch. The glow displayed both hands near twelve. *Midnight. Three days down here, going on four.*

He leaned back against the cool cement. *Cool and dark—like a tomb.* He shuddered at the thought.

As a teen, Peter had read a novel about World War III. When his father noticed him reading it they had a long discussion about what it might really be like. His dad said that after the blast radiation levels fell quickly. But Peter couldn't remember how fast. Would it be safe to leave? Perhaps safe was too strong a term. Would it be possible to leave and survive? He didn't know.

As he thought, sleep overtook him. Images of Sue and Leon drifted into the face of the unseeing old woman in the crowd. Then she dissolved into a mushroom cloud with the face of the devil. In the dream, Peter tried to run from the demon.

With a gasp he awoke to darkness. The sound of shuffling came from the corner where the food and water were stored. Peter wondered if it might be a rat or a large radioactive cockroach. Silently he pulled his flashlight from the belt and turned it on.

The beam revealed Blaine, with a candy bar sticking from his mouth. He fell back against the wall with a thud, slid down and nearly sat on a woman.

"I ... I'm starving," the candy bar thief protested. "You and your friend Anthony have no right to ration the food. It belongs to all of us."

Anthony and several others woke.

A large man stood and grabbed Blaine by the collar. "I was going to eat that candy bar for breakfast." He slammed his fist across Blaine's face.

Thinking that Blaine had been adequately punished, Peter clicked the light off.

After another thud, and a loud moan, Peter flicked the flashlight back on, intending to stop the violence.

The light revealed the big guy moving to a corner with the stub of a candy bar in his mouth. Blaine, with a bloody nose and mouth, crawled the other way.

Peter turned the light off and fell back asleep.

The next morning Blaine kept his bruised face cast down as Anthony served him a half cup of water. He drank it as the others ate the little food that remained.

Peter munched on his half of a candy bar and downed his half glass of water. Then he retreated to his usual spot, near the door.

When he was done handing out the rations, Anthony sat beside him. For several hours they talked, dozed, and talked some more. Gradually the light faded and darkness once again filled the room.

Little more than a whisper, a woman's voice came across the black. "Will anyone look for us? Why hasn't anyone found us?"

"We're already dead," Blaine responded. "You just haven't figured it out."

Someone grunted.

Another cried.

Retrieving the flashlight from his belt Peter aimed it into Blaine's face. "Shut up!" The light faded as the batteries died.

Blaine laughed.

Toward the end of the sixth day, Anthony passed the last half glass of water to each of the nineteen. When he finished, Anthony motioned for Peter to step into the hall. "You said that when the water ran out we would have three days left. Well, we're there. What are we going to do?"

"I don't know. I hoped that searchers would find us. I hoped ...." Peter shook his head. "It doesn't matter what I hoped."

Anthony looked at him expectantly.

Peter turned and walked away.

With no food or drink to break the monotony of the next day the hours crept by. Hunger grew in Peter, but despair and thirst gnawed as darkness fell. By the following morning thirst dominated his thoughts. He imagined drinking, or pouring, water over his head. Peter tried to think of other things. Being in the crowd at a Seahawk's game came to his mind. Images of the players, and the fans in the stadium drifted along, as his thoughts turned to icy cold beer bought at the game.

Fitful sleep overtook him.

The first rays of dawn cast a pale glow over the room; Peter awoke, and wondered what to do.

As if in answer, a woman with black hair, tinged in gray stood. "I'm leaving." She shuffled across the room. "If I'm going to die at least I want to be in the sun." She marched from the room.

Peter nodded as he stood. "I'm going to find help.

Leaning against the gray cement wall a young woman stood. "What should we do?"

"Stay here." Peter moved to the doorway. "If I find help, I'll send them back for all of you."

Blaine laughed. "He's leaving us to die."

"Shut up!" the young woman shouted.

Peter exited and climbed the stairs like a man going to his execution. Sunlight poured in from the large windows on three sides of the lobby. In a pool of light the woman that had left moments earlier sat in a plush executive's chair.

He walked up beside her. A blue sky and yellow sunlight welcomed him. He stood still enjoying more warmth than he had felt in days.

She looked up at him. "I won't go back to that basement."

"I wouldn't ask you to." Peter frowned. "I don't think I ever introduced myself. My name is Peter."

She nodded. "I know. Mine is Debra. How long before I die?"

He shook his head. "I don't know."

Tears welled in her eyes. "If you're not here to take me back then … do you want to join me? There're more chairs like this one."

Peter shook his head. "I'm going to find help."

Debra considered that for a moment. "Do you think you'll find anyone?"

He shrugged. "I've got to try."

"I've got to stay here." Debra turned toward the sunlight.

Peter placed his hand on her shoulder and squeezed. Then he turned and strode out of the building. Almost immediately he encountered the dead.

First his nostrils were hit by the gagging stench of decay. He stepped around the corner and found eight bodies, covered with gray dust, scattered on the sidewalk and pavement. He could only guess how most had died. Several showed evidence of blunt force trauma. *Were they trampled by the crowd?* He shook his head. Others had gunshot wounds.

For some reason he walked to the squad car. Perhaps hoping to find Leon or, more likely, out of habit. Rats scurried away as he approached. Three people lay crumpled and crushed against the rear of the squad car. Staring at the bodies he knew that some emotion should stir within him—horror, outrage, despair, something, but nothing came forth.

Silently, he turned and walked away.

In the shadows a large dog watched him. Two others snarled as they darted across the street in front of him.

Peter rested a hand on his pistol.

He weaved around abandoned cars for nearly a block before he noticed another person, face down in the gutter. Covered with the gray dust that turned everything into a stark moonscape, Peter couldn't tell much more. Something pulled him to the lifeless form. He knelt beside and brushed dust from a sleeve. This person wore a dark uniform. Peter's gut knotted in apprehension. He rolled the body onto its back. His partner, Leon, was dead.

Finally, the tears flowed.

Peter sat in the dust for several minutes. Straining and stumbling he picked up the body of his partner and carried him over his shoulder to a nearby hardware store. Peter kicked the door in and, finding a bench at the back of the store he laid his friend down. Then he collected tarps and duct tape. When he had wrapped and taped Leon in the makeshift shroud, he used a marker to write, "Renton Police Officer, Leon Stewart," on the front.

"I wish I could do more for you." Peter saluted his friend, turned and left.

He knew that any hope of survival depended upon two things. First, he needed to escape the fallout as quickly as possible. Peter decided to follow Highway 99, the major surface street, south as far as he could. Secondly, he needed water, so like an animal in search of prey, his eyes constantly swept right and left hoping to find the life-giving liquid.

As the hours passed, the sun dipped below the nearby buildings, casting long shadows that soon faded into uniform darkness across the powerless city. Still, Peter resisted the idea of finding a place to sleep. He knew that the next day he would reach home and his wife. Only when he stumbled over a body did he relent and find shelter in the stairwell of an apartment building.

Thirst haunted his dreams. He awoke during the night and prowled for water. Nearly crazy with thirst he broke into one apartment after another, checking fridges and pantries. In the fifth apartment he found two bottles. He drank one and fell asleep on the couch.

When the early light of dawn fell across the dead city, Peter awoke. He grinned at the need to pee. Moments later, standing before the toilet, a childhood memory came to him. While still relieving himself, he yanked the lid off the tank and gazed upon several gallons of clean water.

"In an emergency, you can drink this," his father had once told him. Then his dad had taken a cup and drank.

As a ten-year-old, Peter had wanted to appear brave so he followed his dad's example. The water tasted of minerals.

Peter found an empty liter soda bottle in the trash, filled it from the tank, and drank deeply of the cool refreshing waters.

In the pantry he also discovered a few crackers and cookies. Thrilled at the bounty, he found a glass and filled it, then arranged the food like a formal meal before eating. Afterwards, he used a pillowcase as a makeshift pack for his water bottles. Just as he felt ready to continue his journey nausea swept over him, and he ran to the bathroom. Vomiting gave way to dry heaves that left him panting for air on the bathroom floor.

He wondered if dehydration caused the vomiting, but when diarrhea followed he knew the truth. He had left the shelter of the bank basement and paid a price. Even now radiation destroyed the cells of his body. If he didn't find help soon, death would take him. He drank a little more water and this time it stayed with him.

Stepping from the apartment into the morning light, he noticed color had returned to the land. With a smile, he gazed at the blue sky, and the grass in a crack of the sidewalk. Perhaps the water had given him the hope he needed to see it, but the city he walked in today definitely had life and color. Yesterday, he hiked across a world covered with gray fallout. Today, some gray still swirled in the morning breeze, but other colors existed. He stared for over a minute at a green tree and hoped radioactivity wouldn't kill it. He hoped it wouldn't kill him.

Keeping the morning sun on his left, Peter continued south. With each mile he traveled, the buildings shrank from towers, offices and condos to apartments and then individual homes. Fewer abandoned cars littered the roads. Even though the electromagnetic pulse hadn't reached that far south, the residents appeared to have left, or been evacuated.

Am I still walking through radiation?

A few miles ahead a large stream and adjoining lakes divided Kent and Hillcrest. He turned east toward the freeway and the bridge that would take him home. He drank from one of the bottles. If he kept up his present pace he might be home by dusk. He breathed deeply and pushed on.

Exhaustion crept up on him as he moved along unfamiliar streets. At a park he strolled alone across a grassy lawn. In the shade of an old oak tree, he lay atop a picnic table. He should be hungry, but the thought of food made him queasy. He stood, faltered, knelt and retched. When it passed he sipped more water and leaned against the tree. For a moment he felt better, then his gut convulsed and he vomited. The nausea quickly turned to dry heaving.

When it subsided he slid lower, exhausted and unable to move.

Minutes later the sound of vehicles stirred him. Several Humvees sped along the far side of the park and disappeared down a side street.

"Help!" Peter stumbled to his feet, waved and yelled again.

They hadn't heard his feeble cry, but he followed them, on shaky feet, down the slope. Soon his hike took him parallel to the stream and closer to the freeway. When he crested the hill, he fell to his knees in thanks that he might live.

An army post straddled both ends of the bridge below, six Humvees lined the parking lot nearest to him. On the far side of the bridge, a helicopter sat in the middle of another lot being fueled from a tanker truck. A dozen soldiers mingled near a pair of medical tents at the edge of a field.

As he stood, Peter stumbled. Barely staying on his feet, he trudged down the slope, too weak to run.

A man in a biohazard suit came toward him as he neared the army camp. "What's your name?" The man pulled a clipboard from a satchel.

"Peter Westmore."

He looked at the uniform. "You're a police officer?"

Peter nodded.

He pointed. "Well sir, see those civilians standing between the medical tents?"

About a dozen men stood in a wavy line near tarps hanging from poles about ten feet apart. Peter nodded again.

"That's where we're going." The man asked rapid fire questions as they walked. "Next of kin? What's your home address? Social Security number?"

Peter stopped and turned toward the man. "There are other survivors. I went for help."

"I was getting to that question, but okay, we can jump ahead. Where are they?"

Peter gave the address.

Clipboard Man wrote and then pointed. "Get in line here behind the others and you'll be processed."

Women's voices came from the other side of the tarp.

Peter stumbled forward and collapsed to the ground.

Clipboard Man and another person helped him to the front of the line. "We need to get those clothes off you."

As Clipboard helped him undress the other man gave him a plastic bag for his watch, wallet, badge, keys and worthless phone. Still another took his gun.

Peter was too weak to protest.

A soldier checked Peter using a Geiger counter with headphones.

"How bad?" Peter mumbled.

"That's for a doctor to say." Geiger man moved on before Peter could ask another question.

"We need to get you to the showers." Clipboard said.

Peter looked at him with pleading eyes.

"I don't know how sick you are, but you will be told." Clipboard helped him stand. "The shower will help."

Leaning against a rough wooden wall he let the water pour onto him while others scrubbed him with coarse brushes. As he dried himself with a towel, hair drifted in the air. He ran moist fingers along his head, and a dozen strands clung to it. *This can't be good.*

A second person checked him with a Geiger counter, and he answered more questions.

Exhausted and barely able to stand, Peter leaned on a soldier as they walked to the medical tent. There Peter collapsed upon a cot.

Only as his eyes blinked open did he realize he had slept. A line of lightbulbs along the apex of the long tent cast a dim glow over the two rows of patients. An IV bag hung beside him and a tube ran to his left arm. Someone had hung a plastic bag to one corner of the cot. Inside were all his personal items, except his pistol. A look under the blankets revealed he wore only a thin hospital gown.

Moving just his head he looked about. Peter's cot stood at one end of the tent near the entrance on his right. A cool breeze flowed in through an open tent flap. On the left lay another patient. Blood stained bandages wrapped most of his head. Patches covered his eyes. His mouth hung open.

Is he asleep or dead?

Nearby another wore even bloodier bandages over his head, chest, and arms. He muttered and moaned.

Suffering only weakness, a headache and vomiting, Peter felt strangely fortunate. Could he, should he, pray for God's help in his personal quest in the midst of such suffering?

God if you can't help me, keep Sue and our son safe.

He dozed, but when he awoke two doctors stood just outside the tent. The older man wore the uniform of an army colonel, the younger wore civilian clothes.

"All the patients inside left the contaminated zone in the last twenty-four hours." The colonel gestured toward Peter's tent. "They all have significant radiation poisoning."

Peter held still with his eyes barely open, pretending to sleep.

The younger doctor glanced in Peter's direction. "What are we doing for them?"

"Treating symptoms and waiting for a hospital bed to open up." The colonel shook his head. "The prognosis for all of them is grim."

The young doctor shook his head. "So many have died."

The colonel nodded, and then turned and walked away.

The younger man entered and stepped to the patient across the way from Peter. None of the patients stirred as he moved from one to the next reading charts.

Peter needed to hear the full extent of his condition. When the young doctor reached for his chart, Peter said, "I guess you've been a very busy man these last few days, Dr. Harper."

The man stepped back, eyes wide. "Ah well, yes." His smile looked forced. "The first day there were hundreds of people, maybe thousands. I lost count." He shook his head. "But the last couple of days there haven't been many."

"Hopefully they got out."

"Search teams are finding a lot of bodies."

Peter sighed. "I walked out of the contaminated area to find help for a group of survivors. Will I live?"

The doctor looked at his chart. "Oh, you're the one they were talking about earlier, the police officer who reported the location of sixteen others when he arrived." He pulled a chair near Peter's cot and sat.

"There were nineteen ... well eighteen after I left. Were they okay?"

"From what I heard sixteen will be. That's a great accomplishment to get that many safely out of the contaminated zone."

Peter thought of Leslie and the baby she carried, of Anthony and Debra from the bank. He nodded and hoped they were all okay. "How about me? Will I be okay?"

"Ah." The doctor looked at the chart.

"Give it to me straight, doc. I need to know."

"It's clear you're experiencing radiation sickness, and that you breathed in some fallout, ingested it or both. That complicates your recovery."

"Will I recover?"

For a moment the doctor remained silent. "Is there a loved one we should contact?"

"With a little help from you, I'll take care of that."

When Dr. Harper returned the next morning, rays of sunshine provided only scant light. In his right hand he carried a white plastic garbage bag.

Seeing him, Peter pulled the blankets back, sat up, and dropped his feet to the tarpaulin floor beneath his cot.

"Slow down." The young doctor made a stop motion with one hand. "I want to examine you first."

Peter sat on the edge of the cot, anxious to start his journey.

After an examination, the doctor shook his head. "Your heart rate and pulse remain strong. Your breathing is normal, but your symptoms, fatigue, nausea, diarrhea, and hair loss, they tell me you've had significant radiation exposure."

Peter slumped. "I'm sure that's so."

Dr. Harper reached for the nearby chart and made notes "The best professional advice I can give is to remain here and receive treatment."

"Treatment?"

"Well … ah." Harper looked at the chart and then his feet.

"Can you cure me?" Will I live?"

"There is no cure. We could only treat the symptoms and your ultimate prognosis is not good."

Peter nodded and took a deep breath. "Are you married?" Peter gripped the IV pole and stood.

"Engaged. Why?"

"In my situation what would you do? Stay here and probably die, or find your loved ones and ...." Peter shrugged. "I want to find my wife. The rest is in God's hands."

Dr. Harper nodded. "That's what I expected." He handed the bag to Peter. "These are used clothes from the Salvation Army. Also inside are a couple of water bottles and MREs and this." The doctor held up a container of pills. "For the nausea." He put everything except the clothes back in the bag. "Get dressed. I hope everything fits. I'll go make transportation arrangements."

"Can I get my gun back, or get another one?"

"Sorry, I don't have access to weapons." Harper turned and hurried off.

Standing, pulling on pants and socks, all took more effort, and time than he expected, but the thought of going home invigorated him. He clutched the plastic bag with his personal things and continued getting ready. He had barely finished when Dr. Harper returned.

"Good." He waved for Peter to follow. "I want you on your way before anyone discovers you're gone."

Grabbing the trash bag containing the water bottles, food and pills, Peter followed.

Outside the doctor pointed to a line of vehicles along the shoulder of the highway. "They're headed south for supplies. They'll take you to the exit you mentioned last night. From there you're on your own."

Peter grasped the doctor's hand. "Thanks."

"I'll go along, and introduce you to the convoy commander."

Together they walked toward the vehicles, two-hundred yards away. About halfway there Peter stumbled over a stone.

Harper grabbed him with both hands.

Peter steadied himself and stepped forward.

"Doctor Harper, what's going on here?"

Peter and the doctor turned at the sound of the colonel's voice.

"This man should be in the hospital tent."

"Yes sir, well ... ah," Dr. Harper grimaced.

Peter stood tall. "I'm going home to my wife. I'd like to ride south with the convoy, but with or without it, I'm headed south."

The colonel stared at him for a moment, and then nodded. "You're the police officer, aren't you? The one that saved the sixteen others."

"Yes, sir."

For a moment the two faced each other. Then the colonel nodded. "The convoy will take you as far as they can. I hope you find her." He turned and walked away.

Dr. Harper led Peter to the Lieutenant in charge of the convoy.

"Sure, Harper mentioned you need a ride. We can take you to that exit," the officer said. "But from what I've been told, the Hillcrest area has been evacuated."

"I need to try and find her."

"Okay, get in the last truck." The officer pointed. "I'll tell the driver what to do."

With the doctor's help, Peter climbed in. As the trucks started south, he waved goodbye and thanked the young man who helped him.

For the next thirty minutes Peter exchanged stories with the driver and gazed at the highway, streets, and nearby buildings. Even this far south, fire had blackened entire neighborhoods and smoke still drifted in the air. Yet, most remained familiar, but now so vacant, lifeless and empty. Peter prayed his home had not been burned. "There's my exit."

The driver nodded, and steered to the off ramp that sloped up to the cross street. He stopped at the intersection and held out his hand. "Good luck. I hope you find her."

Peter shook his hand, thanked him, and stepped from the truck. He took a deep breath and trudged east on a slow hike into Hillcrest. It had always been a quick drive from the freeway to his house, but he had never walked it—or measured the distance. Still, he decided to follow the same route he would have driven.

For several blocks he kept a good pace through the uninhabited world. Only looted stores and the smoke that irritated his throat, hinted at the true nature of the disaster.

His pace slowed as he noticed the gradual incline of the road and his own faster breathing. He had never thought about it before, but Hillcrest had been aptly named. He rested for several minutes, drank water, took a deep breath, and forced his feet forward.

Later, he reached the large church building that dominated the surrounding area and blocked his view of the homes beyond. On warm Sunday mornings he and Sue had walked to the church for services. Now that hike seemed endless.

Peter left the road and cut across the church parking lot. As he rounded the building, he stopped and slid to his knees. A neighborhood of charred rubble stood before him. Only concrete, chimneys and burnt wood remained.

Had Sue seen all this? Had she survived? Peter drank more water and pushed along, up the hill toward home.

A few minutes later he reached the road where the fire stopped. He crossed the pavement to unburnt homes. Some had been looted, windows and doors were broken, furniture and clothes scattered on lawns.

Sick with fear for his wife and son, he pushed onward to the main thoroughfare at the top of the ridge. His destination, the end of his journey, lay less than a mile away. Breathing hard he tried to jog, but after a half dozen paces returned to a slower pace. He weaved around abandoned cars leaning on each as he did. Several blocks passed as strength drained from his legs.

Then, on the left, he saw the familiar cul-de-sac. With waning will, he jogged around the corner, and spotted their two-story peach home. Someone had broken the living room window and trash littered the lawn, but it was home.

"Sue! Sue!" Using all his strength, he hurried onward, shouting her name.

His heart pounding, he climbed the steps to the front door on legs that wobbled like those of an old man. A boot print marred the paint near the deadbolt. He reached for his gun that wasn't there. Silently he placed his hand on the door and pushed it open with a squeak.

Sue had asked him to oil the hinges.

Stepping into the living room, he noticed the couch near the door. The television, a recliner, and end table, were gone. In the kitchen many cabinets stood open. Flatware lay scattered on the floor. Clothes hung from the dryer. All of that didn't matter.

"Sue?" He said her name tentatively. Then he changed his plan. "This is Sergeant Peter Westmore with the Renton Police Department. I'm looking for survivors. Are there any in this house?" He prayed to hear Sue's voice, but no sound came back to him. He repeated the message as he moved through the first floor.

Sue had not answered him. Either she had gone or she couldn't ...." No he would not go down that line of thought. Heart pounding, he trudged up the stairs.

The hallway stood clear of debris. He opened the first upstairs door, a small bedroom they used for storage. It appeared undisturbed, but he conducted a quick search, and then moved down the hall.

He didn't want to open the next door. For nearly a minute he leaned against the wall listening to his heavy breathing. When he did enter the room only blue walls, dinosaurs, sea creatures and infant furniture greeted him. A quick search of what would have been the nursery revealed nothing. His heart ached.

Why had the looters not gone upstairs? "Sue, where are you? He inched toward the master bedroom. "Are you alive? Did you go to Mom and Dad's place?"

He opened the door to the master bedroom. A king-size bed, neatly made, with a pastel blue bedspread stood opposite him. On his side of the room, stood the antique roll-top desk where he paid the bills. It had been in the spare bedroom, but that was now the nursery. Across the room from the desk stood the dresser. Everything looked as if he had just come home from work on a normal day.

Then he noticed the bullet holes in the wall. The two holes were in a close pattern about three feet up the wall from the floor. Peter bent over and touched them. No blood stained the wall or the floor. What had happened here? Fear pounded in his chest.

He had pushed so hard to get there, but he had lost the fight to find his family. His knees buckled and he collapsed to the floor. Sue and his unborn child were gone. "Help me, God. Tell me where they are, please. Did they go with Dad? Please, I need to know." Peter wept.

Later, when tears had passed, he stood, stumbled and fell across the bed. Exhausted, he slept. When he awoke, twilight filled the room. A check of his watch showed that dawn would soon arrive. He dozed in the waning darkness waiting for light. When enough flowed through the window he stood on wobbly legs. Looking down, he noticed mottled bruises on his lower arms. The two around the IV needle spots did not surprise him, but the dozen others confirmed what he already knew. The radiation sickness would soon take him. Fatigued, he collapsed into a chair.

"Is Sue alive?" he asked in a quavering voice. "Our son? Please God, I've got to know. Did Dad come and take them to Hansen? Let Sue and our son live. Give them a chance."

Peter slumped deep into the cushioned chair. From the plastic bag, he retrieved a water bottle and drank without regard for the future. He took a couple of the pills and set them on the nightstand. Then he ate the last of his food.

The nourishment gave him no vigor. He felt certain this day would be his last. He considered that awareness a gift. Not many people knew the day of their death, but what would he do with that knowledge?

Drowsiness gripped him, but he fought it, fearful he would not awaken. As he contemplated his final hours a fly buzzed across the room and landed on the desk beside him. There, two antique glass paperweights, and a pen, held down a scribbled note. He looked closer. The swirls and flourishes were the quick handwriting of Sue. Eyes filling with tears, he leaned close to read it.

My Dearest Peter

I am well and pray that you are too. Your father came for me. I'll be waiting for you at the farm. Come quickly.

All my love,

Sue

She lived! He laughed with all his remaining strength. Then he reread the note and read it once again. He thought about finding a working car and driving to the farm, but he knew that he lacked the strength. Gradually a plan formed.

Peter staggered to the closet and found his dress uniform still shrouded in plastic from the cleaners. He was a police officer and would rather die in uniform than clothes from charity. Thirty minutes later he stood in front of the mirror properly dressed and feeling his life draining from him like sweat from pores.

He sat at the desk with a thud and pushed bills and paperweights out of the way. He retrieved paper, envelopes, and clutched the pen Sue had left behind. As he wrote, tears welled in his eyes and fell on the page.

To whoever finds this;

My name is Peter Westmore. I am a sergeant with the Renton Police Department assisting the Seattle P.D. with the evacuation before the blast. We didn't know where or when the bomb would go off, but when it did I knew immediately that I was too close. The roads were clogged before the blast. The growing mushroom cloud, storm of dust and snow-like fallout only made it worse.

The doctor at the medical station told me what I already knew; the dose of radiation I received is lethal. They wanted to keep me at the medical facility, but I didn't want to die there. I needed to find my wife and make sure she was safe.

By the time I reached the house it was deserted and I am too weak to go on. Please, whoever finds this, get the enclosed letter to my family in Hansen. The address is on the envelope.

Peter Westmore

Weak from writing, he struggled to keep his hand steady, and the words of his final note, neat.

Dearest Sue,

I found your note. It fills me with happiness to know that Dad reached you. I prayed that he would.

Please don't cry that I couldn't follow you to the farm. Raise our son, and enjoy every day of the life you have. I'll be waiting in heaven when you arrive.

I'm sorry I couldn't be there to love and protect you, but if possible I'll watch over you and our boy. If I can, I'll be near you, at least on those important days,

Christmas, birthdays, and our anniversary. But if that cannot be, when you get to heaven we'll have forever together and you can tell me what I missed.

Until that glorious day when we're together again,

Love, Peter.

The pen dropped from his shaking hand. As exhaustion swept over him he enclosed the letter for Sue in an envelope and wrote her name on it. Then he folded the note for "whoever finds this," around another and placed both in the small plastic food bag. Slowly he laid on the bed he had shared with Sue as images of her and their unborn son filled his mind. A final tear rolled down his cheek as he thought of all they might have shared, all that might have been. With a slight shake of his head he rejected sadness. He had known her, loved her, and she would live, along with their son. That was enough.

Still clutching the bag with the letters, a smile came to his face as he closed his eyes forever.

The Long Way Home

The Long way home is a 20,000 word novella set within the framework of Through Many Fires, *the first novel in the* Strengthen What Remains *series. Shortly after the release of* Through Many Fires *I began receiving emails asking for a fuller account of how Trevor brought Sue home to the farm. This is the complete story. Fans of the series have already read a parallel account of the resolution in chapters 22 and 23 of* Through Many Fires.

Day 1, February 7th.

Everywhere chaos and panic grew. Trevor held the hand of his wife, Sarah. Together they stood on the porch and stared down the long gravel driveway in a vigil of waiting. He knew her heart yearned to see their children home and safe on the farm, because his own heart ached for the same, but what could he do?

After several minutes he turned to her. "Start breakfast. I'll get the eggs this morning." He put on a blue denim jacket, grabbed a small pail and, not wanting to be away from her for long, strode toward the barn. A gray February sky produced a gentle snow that mostly melted as it touched the ground.

These last few days Trevor watched as Sarah threw herself into the tasks of home and farm. Each time she paused worry etched her face. He needed to be there with her to give comfort, but he had little to give.

In particular, he hurt for the son farthest away, and perhaps already gone. They hadn't heard from Caden since before the attack on Washington, DC. He would have been in or near the city when the terrorists set off the bomb that destroyed it. If his son died that day, Trevor hoped it had been quick and painless.

Peter, their eldest son, had phoned yesterday. Every officer in the police department would be doing twelve-hour shifts until the emergency passed.

"Do you want Sue to come and stay with us until this is over?" Trevor asked.

"Yes, but she won't." Peter sighed. "Sue insists upon staying in our house … says she wants to be home when I get there."

The call ended with Peter's promise to phone when he could.

Their third child, Lisa, also troubled his heart. Only eighty miles away at college, she should have already been home, but in the growing chaos, they had lost touch with her.

In the barn, he filled the pail with mash and cracked corn, and then moved to the henhouse. He emptied the container into the feeders and collected thirteen eggs back into the pail.

As he entered through the side door of the house, Trevor heard his wife talking.

"It's Peter! He wants to speak with you."

Only one phone had ever been installed in the old farmhouse and now, Sarah hesitated as she passed the receiver to him and sat nearby.

"Hello, Peter, it's good to hear from you."

"Hi, Dad. I wish I had more time. I need you to take Sue to the farm."

"But, you said she wouldn't—."

"Make her go, Dad. There isn't much time until…."

As Peter's voice faded, Trevor understood his unstated meaning. A terrorist cell must have been discovered in Seattle. In other cities, if the authorities hadn't acted quickly, the terrorists had set off nuclear blasts that killed hundreds of thousands. Before Trevor responded, the line went dead. Fearing the worst, he looked out the window, expecting a flash of light, but saw only the cloudy skies of February. After a moment he hung up the phone and turned to Sarah. "I've got to go."

"Where?"

"I'm going to get Sue, and hopefully I'll find Lisa." He jogged into the living room, pulled his go-bag from the closet, and set it by the front door. When he turned to kiss Sarah, her eyes were wide, lips pursed, and face pale. Trevor's resolve faded as he embraced her.

For a long moment Sarah rested her head on his chest. Then she looked into his eyes. "Go. Bring our family home." She nodded. "You've got to do this, but before you go I'll make you a good breakfast—."

"That I can take with me."

She nodded. "And a mug of coffee."

He clutched her hand for a moment before proceeding.

While Sarah prepared the food, he hefted the go-bag and set it in the back of the cab of his old Ford F-250 pickup. He had enough gas in the tank to make the trip, but as a precaution he retrieved a dented five-gallon metal gas can, normally used to fill farm equipment, and put it in the back of the truck. He donned his camo hunting jacket, selected a twelve gauge shotgun, and set it, along with a box of ammo, on the go-bag.

Sarah walked from the house holding an old gray lunch pail and the mug of coffee.

He took them, leaned down, and one last time before departing, he hugged and kissed Sarah.

"I'll be back soon."

"You better." The sad smile of parting grew on her face. "And bring Sue and Lisa with you."

He nodded, climbed into the truck and turned the key. Despite the cold, the engine fired up on the first try. He slid the vehicle into gear and the old red monster rumbled down the driveway, and on toward the freeway.

He had come of age after the Vietnam War. While he had enlisted in the army, and served four years, his life had largely been as a farmer and without violent conflict. Still, he asked Sarah to stock up on food. They kept chickens, grew assorted fruit trees, and kept preparing.

Trevor had learned to shoot as a boy, improved the skill in the army, and continued to refine his talent over time. He had learned ammo reloading, basic carpentry, plumbing, and other useful skills. Now he hoped that those prepper skills, which had been largely a lifestyle choice, would save him and his family as the country descended into chaos.

Few cars headed north, like Trevor, toward Seattle and the terrorists, but the southbound lanes inched along as a solid mass of vehicles. Dozens of motorcycles drove along the edges and the median. Many crossed to his side of the road where they could, and drove the wrong way. Trevor swerved to avoid them. Others weren't so nimble. He lost count of the crumpled and burning vehicles along the median of the highway.

As he headed north, wrong-way drivers became less of a problem due to the concrete barrier in the middle of the interstate. Pedestrians were now the greater hazard. On the other side of the road, hordes of people walked south amid the nearly motionless cars. Both sides of the highway brimmed with foot traffic, and many used the nearly empty northbound lanes as a wide sidewalk. Trevor weaved his way north as he gawked at a world gone mad.

Approaching an overpass, just south of the state capital, a line of police cars blocked the freeway. Officers directed traffic onto the side streets.

Trevor slowed to a stop.

"Keep moving," a nearby officer ordered as he pointed to the off ramp. "The freeway is closed ahead."

"I'm headed to Hillcrest to bring my——."

"You'll need to use the surface streets. We're opening both sides of the interstate to southbound traffic."

Trevor sighed. He didn't have one of those new phones with a GPS, and his pickup lacked any electronics newer than a radio. He leaned over and retrieved an ancient paper map from the glove compartment, before exiting the freeway.

On the narrower, two-lane streets, Trevor felt like a man standing in a slow motion cattle stampede. Cars, trucks, and people weaved in and out using both sides of the road to make whatever progress they could. Trevor zig-zagged left and right, and through parking lots as drizzle, mixed with light snow, made the journey all the more dangerous. However, as he banged, bumped, and pushed north, away from the freeway, traffic thinned. Still, driving demanded absolute attention. Cars weaved wildly and only reluctantly stopped at, or more often in, intersections. Repeatedly they ignored yellow lights. Pedestrians ran across roads.

Traffic inched forward for several minutes, but then halted. Trevor turned into a store parking lot, and drove diagonally across to a side street he'd never before used. For several blocks he continued north using the sun to maintain his course.

A bang, crunch, and scrape of metal on metal, caused Trevor to look down the line of vehicles. A fuel truck blocked the intersection ahead. Traffic stopped.

Trevor braked, leaving space between him and the sedan ahead of him. Somehow he would need to circumvent this obstruction. A glance at his watch confirmed what he already thought; no trip to Peter and Sue's home had ever taken this long. He pulled papers from the glovebox until he found a pencil. Using his pocket knife, he carved a new point while studying the map. He marked his destination, and then, unfolded the chart another flap, and circled the university where he hoped to find Lisa.

"Get back!" a man yelled.

Trevor's head shot up from his map as a thunderous boom shook the pickup. The tanker truck had exploded into a rolling ball of flame. Heat slapped his face.

Screams mixed with the wail of horns and screeching tires.

He twisted the steering wheel sharply to the right, hit the gas, and bounced up onto the sidewalk and into the parking lot of a fast food restaurant. A glance in his rearview mirror revealed others followed him or used their vehicles to push burning cars out of the way and escape the growing inferno.

Exiting the parking lot, Trevor drove down a nearly empty side street, turned left and soon continued north toward Hillcrest.

Using unfamiliar side streets more than an hour passed before he reached the long arcing road that swept north past the church Peter and Sue attended. Trevor followed it to the last major street he would need to cross on the way to his son's home. However, as he neared the boulevard clogged with traffic, he saw no way forward. Motorists ignored the stoplight and pushed into the intersection, creating an obstruction of steel and aluminum.

Trevor stared at the slow moving traffic that frustrated his progress. When the light turned green he crept forward until he almost touched the Cadillac coupe that blocked his way.

The woman in the passenger seat gazed at him with frightened eyes.

"Don't worry," Trevor whispered to himself. "It's the next vehicle I intend to cutoff." He turned and locked eyes with the driver immediately behind the Cadillac. That guy, in a Honda Civic, seemed to understand. The young man, with brown hair pulled tightly back on his head, inched forward to the rear bumper of the caddy and then used a very impolite gesture.

Trevor smiled, shifted into first gear, but kept his foot on the clutch and brake.

The Caddy inched through the intersection untouched.

Trevor stared at the traffic signal. It still glowed green for him, but all the drivers, including the young man in the Civic, ignored it.

When the Honda reached the right spot, Trevor released his pedals. The steel of the old pickup pressed against the much lighter Honda and, like a police pit maneuver, pushed it away.

Horns blared.

A pony tail bounced on the shoulder of the Honda driver as he jumped from his car.

Trevor locked the pickup door and lifted a pistol from the bag beside him. Making motions with his gun hand, he signaled that he only wanted to cross the street.

Ponytail guy's eyes flared wide as his face turned crimson. He backed away. Other drivers shouted and honked, but gradually Trevor pushed and weaved across.

As he pulled out of the intersection on the north side, he let out a deep breath then sucked in cool air. Sweat trickled down his forehead. He pressed the accelerator, anxious to leave the angry motorists behind.

Trevor continued north, and slightly downhill, passing cars packed with people and belongings. On both sides of the street, homes had broken windows and half open doors. After several blocks, he came to a turn on the left. He pressed the gas and, in his hurry, turned in front of an oncoming car.

The other driver braked. Tires squealed and a horn blared.

Trevor pressed harder on the accelerator. The truck fishtailed, gained traction, and raced up the side street.

With an angry shout, the other driver sped on his way.

The noise of traffic continued as Trevor sped from the main avenue, toward his destination.

Moments later he spotted the cul-de-sac. There, up ahead, stood the two-story peach-colored home of Peter and Sue. About a half dozen families along the road hurriedly prepared to leave. Men crammed boxes in cars as they cast Trevor a wary eye. Children cried. Women scurried about. As he came to a stop in the driveway, he examined the front of the house. It appeared undisturbed. Still, he clutched his pistol and took the keys as he exited the truck.

Sound from a television inside the house could be heard over the cacophony of chaos on the street. Hopeful, he pressed the doorbell and knocked.

The television droned on.

He shouted for Sue, but heard no reply. He didn't expect Peter to be home, but still he called his name.

He walked around the house, checking doors and windows. All were locked. Once again, at the front door he pondered whether to leave. No. He had driven all this way. He needed to know for certain that Sue was not there.

Stepping back, he raised his right leg, and with all his might kicked the door.

It popped open, but only a few inches. Trevor noticed he left a boot print on the door and the wood around the strike plate had splintered. He shook his head. The door opened too easily for all that breakage. Nevertheless he resolved to fix the frame, and paint the door, when things returned to normal.

He pushed the door open enough to get his head in. The couch stood against it. Leaning against the door, he pushed it the rest of the way open. "Sue? It's Trevor." Sweeping the pistol slowly before him he looked about. "Are you here?" Trevor called in a low voice.

He stepped to the center of the living room. A recliner and end table were missing.

"Sue?" he called in a loud voice. "Peter sent me."

Clearly the couch had been moved.

A reporter on television conveyed the latest news about the Seattle terror cell, gridlock on the roads, and looting. He looked for the remote to turn it off, but couldn't find it.

Would he be able to hear Sue over the television beside him, and the sirens, shouts, sobs and honking outside?

Still leading with the pistol, he moved to the kitchen and laundry room. Every cabinet stood open. Clothes spilled from the dryer.

Returning to the base of the stairs, he considered what he had found. A television on, and someone recently doing chores, but the house partially looted. Had Sue fled from the home when people broke in?

"Sue? Are you here?" He tried to sound calm, even conversational.

Taking one step at a time, he climbed the stairs.

The second floor hallway appeared neat and tidy.

The first room he reached had been used as a storeroom. No sheets covered the bed, boxes stood in the corner and were stacked in the open closet.

From a visit three weeks ago, he recalled that the next room would be the nursery. He opened the door. Peter had been busy. Blue wallpaper, with dinosaurs and sea creatures, covered what had been plain white walls.

His eyes rested on the playpen, diapers, bottles and stockpiled baby items. When he found Sue, he would load the supplies and furniture into the truck.

He left the nursery, and opened the bathroom door. The shower curtain was drawn. Silently he moved forward. "Sue, this is Trevor. Peter sent me. Are you in here?" He yanked the curtain. The rod fell to the floor.

The tub stood empty.

Thud.

The sound came from the bedroom.

Trevor held his breath as he crept from the guest bathroom to the master bedroom. If Sue was in there, she should have answered him. His gut churned with fear. "Sue?" he whispered. "Peter?"

Trevor heard movement as he slowly turned the knob. Then he flung the door open, and followed with his pistol in the lead. "Sue? Are you in here? It's Trevor."

From his right, Trevor heard a gasp, and turned.

Sitting in the corner, a wide-eyed Sue held a gun pointed at him.

Trevor stepped back and raised both hands. "It's okay. It's me, Trevor."

Tears rolled down her cheeks. The hand with the pistol slumped to the floor. "I thought it sounded like you, but I was afraid." She sighed. "Peter said you might come, but then I couldn't reach him … or you … hours passed and then the looters."

Dropping his hands, he stepped closer. "Looters? Is that what happened downstairs? Are you okay?"

"Men broke in last night. I was in the bedroom. I got Peter's handgun and …." She pointed to a spot behind Trevor.

Two bullet holes were in the wall behind him. "You did that?" He reached out to her.

She nodded and clasped his hand and tried to stand. "My leg is asleep … and then of course my big belly gets in the way."

Trevor used both hands to help her stand and briefly they clung to each other.

"I'm glad you're here," She sat on the neatly made king-size bed,

"I'm glad I found you. So, after you shot did the looters leave?"

"Oh, they left in a hurry! But when I finally went downstairs the front door was broken. The deadbolt wouldn't latch … lock or whatever. I tried to move the couch against the door, but couldn't. So I came back here and phoned Peter, and you, a dozen times, but couldn't get through, so I've just been waiting for him."

"He called me a few hours ago. Grab what you need." Trevor swept his arm around the room. "We're getting out of here."

"No." She shook her head. "I should wait for Peter."

"He told me to get you."

A flash of light filled the room.

Trevor pulled Sue tight to his chest. "Close your eyes!" He clamped his own shut, but a blood red glow shined through.

When the light faded, a deep, roaring boom rattled the glass like a stormy day.

Trevor ran to a window. An angry cloud rose in the sky to the north. Lightning flashed. "We've got to go!"

"But—."

"No buts. Grab what you need." Trevor looked about. "Does Peter have a go-bag?"

"A what?"

Trevor looked about. "A duffle bag with supplies."

She nodded. "First floor. In the entryway closet."

Taking her hand, Trevor moved toward the door.

"No, I've got to leave him a note."

"Okay, but be quick." He hurried downstairs and found the bag, but hesitated to take it. If Peter came home he'd need the supplies.

Thunder and a deep rumbling rattled the house.

Caden had probably died in Washington DC. His daughter, Lisa, remained missing. Had Peter just died a few miles to the north? Were all his children dead?

Sue waddled downstairs wearing tennis shoes and a light jacket. She carried two baby bags over one shoulder and a suitcase bumped down the stairs behind her.

Peter's wife and son will live! He grabbed the go-bag and took the suitcase from Sue. "Let's go!"

Outside, Sue stared as the cloud rose over a line of trees to the north. Lightning flashed in different parts of the sky. "Peter." Tears rolled down her cheeks and she held her belly.

Shouts, screams, and cries echoed from the nearby cars and homes.

Clutching her hand, Trevor pulled her to the pickup. "Come on, we've got to move!" Once she was in, he shut the passenger door and hurried to the other side. He turned the key and the engine roared. Tires squealed as they shot out of the driveway and down the road.

They sped toward the main intersection at the top of the hill where Trevor had crossed minutes earlier. He slowed as he looked for a way through the clogged street.

"They're not moving," Sue said.

"The cars? They're blocked in."

"Some are blocked, but none of them are moving."

Trevor looked up and down the street. Sue was right, only one vehicle on the road moved—his pickup, and like a zombie horde, dozens of people ran toward them.

"Lock your door." Trevor pushed the button down on his side. All lanes of the freeway were probably now open to southbound traffic. But the electromagnetic pulse had disabled many cars. Images of stalled vehicles stretching for miles coursed through his mind. Trevor thanked God for his old farm truck with a distributor, carburetor, and no critical electronic parts.

The intersection ahead remained blocked. He could push through, he had done it once before, but while he maneuvered, his truck would be surrounded by a frightened mob. He needed to keep moving. A plan coalesced in his mind. "Brace yourself." He veered into the other lane and raced back the way they had come. "Do you know the way to the North Road?"

"Yes." Sue held onto the shoulder strap like it was a lifeline.

Trevor darted around a stopped sedan. "Give me directions." He glanced at her.

Sue screamed and pointed straight ahead.

A man in a suit and tie, stood in the road with a pistol pointed at them.

Fear mixed with anger as Trevor stomped on the gas.

The well-dressed man jumped but, with a thud, bounced off the side and onto the pavement.

Trevor drove on.

"Oh … my … God!" Sue cried with each word louder than the previous. "Should we stop … call 911 or something?"

"You can call, but we aren't stopping." Trevor pushed guilty thoughts about hit and run aside and resisted the urge to look in the rearview mirror. He swerved around a couple trying to cross the road as others darted about. "Directions! Give me directions."

"Ahhhh." Sue set down her phone without calling, clutched the seat-belt strap with one hand and pointed with the other. "Turn at that street up there."

"Right or left, Sue? I've got to keep my eyes on the road."

"Right."

Tires squealed as the truck turned east. Almost immediately they crossed an overpass. The freeway wasn't quite as he imagined. The vehicles did form a logjam, but motorcycles and pedestrians weaved among the still vehicles.

In similar fashion, Trevor twisted and turned the truck past disabled cars, and frightened people. As they drove, a few vehicles pulled in behind them. Did they think he knew the way to safety?

Beyond the EMP zone, dozens of cars and trucks hurried along side streets, through parking lots and across lawns. All shared an urgency to leave the blast area, disabled vehicles and the terrified mob.

Gradually, Sue's breathing slowed. "I'll be glad when we get to the farm."

"Yeah, but we're not there yet," Trevor mumbled. "What's that up ahead?"

"The bridge is the city limit. The road narrows there from two lanes each way to one."

Cars, some crumpled and bent, others with owners trying to start them, clogged the tiny span across the creek.

The stoplight ahead stood dark. "Maybe the freeway is clear farther south." Trevor swerved right at the next intersection.

"Oh!" Sue shouted. "Try and warn me."

"Sorry." Trevor swerved around a young boy in the road.

"I'm lost." Sue's head shifted right, left and back as they passed the child. "Where are you going?"

"I'm trying Highway 7 south, it looks less congested, and then we'll see how traffic is on the freeway." He weaved past two stalled cars. "I'm just looking for the best route away from here." As they continued south, the vehicles all seemed to be working. Trevor relaxed his grip on the steering wheel and rubbed his sore neck.

About forty yards ahead a man, holding a gas can, sprinted from a car. Almost at once, a teen ran to the vehicle and yanked a bike from a rack at the rear. Shouts, shots and screams followed. The bike thief collapsed to the pavement as a crowd formed.

Trevor pressed hard on the gas pedal, and hurtled past the mob.

Sue exhaled deeply, and slumped in the seat.

"Are you okay?"

Her eyes were closed with both hands resting on her large belly. "Yeah, I think so."

Ahead, vehicles on Highway 7 stood motionless due to an accident. Trevor turned onto side streets and traveled west, then south, and finally east trying to move away from the blast area. Two hours later he turned back on to Highway 7.

At the sound of aircraft, Trevor looked up. A dozen military helicopters flew single file overhead. In the distance, planes and copters flew back and forth. "We must be near the military base."

With eyes still closed, Sue mumbled, "Lewis-McChord?"

Trevor nodded. "Yeah, to the west I would guess."

The truck bounced through several pot holes.

"Oh … ah, could we slow down?" Sue grabbed the handle, rolled down the window and vomited.

"What's wrong?" Trevor's gaze darted between Sue and the road. He worried that she might have been exposed to radiation. Perhaps they both had been. "Are you ill?"

"I don't know, maybe." She breathed deep and slow. "Do you have some water?"

"Yeah, a half dozen plastic bottles in the camo bag behind you."

She drank several mouthfuls and took a deep breath. "I feel lightheaded."

"Should I stop?"

"No. I'll be okay."

"Ah … we'll be at the farm soon." He hoped.

She nodded, pulled to loosen the belt under her belly, and slumped low in the seat.

Trevor continued to bounce along the back-country highway as night fell on a darkened world. He hadn't thought about it earlier, but with the blast and EMP, the power had probably failed over a large portion of western Washington.

As the night grew deeper, Highway 7 changed to 507, but Trevor only noticed after it had occurred. He couldn't recall the exact directions, but felt certain they continued generally south.

Only as they passed did Trevor notice the gas station. All the lights were off, as were the lights of every other building, and he doubted they had any gas.

Rounding a corner, Trevor spotted lights and slowed down. Military tents stood along the river with Humvees and trucks parked alongside. He eyed a checkpoint at the bridge and continued to slow with the other vehicles.

Sue sat up. Looking about, she asked, "What's going on?"

"Some sort of checkpoint at the Nisqually River. I think they're stopping people from going north."

"We're going south, right?"

"Yeah." Trevor nodded. "We should be fine. The traffic is just slower here." Moments later he spotted a large tent with a red cross and pulled off the road.

Sue looked at him, clearly confused. "Why are we stopping?"

Trevor pointed to the medical tent. "Vomiting, fatigue, dizziness, and a nuclear blast. I'm worried about you."

"It's not the blast, I'm pregnant."

"This shouldn't take long and besides, I need to put some gas in the truck."

Vehicles continued across the bridge, but a few cars pulled off. A man ran toward the tent carrying a small child with a blood-stained shirt. An obviously pregnant woman waddled by with her face in a grimace.

Sue leaned close to Trevor. "Those people need to be here, not me."

Trevor retrieved the five-gallon can from the back of the truck.

Sue leaned against the vehicle while he poured the gas into the tank.

"Come on. If they can't see you we'll leave." Trevor locked the truck and gestured toward the medical tent.

Sue trudged to the entrance. "One of the worst things about being pregnant is having doctors poke and prod your private parts."

"I don't think that's what will be happening here."

"Good."

Trevor already regretted his decision to stop, but didn't know when, with the current chaos, they might be this close to medical care. It would give him peace of mind to know they both were fine.

Just outside the tent, a soldier holding a Geiger counter waved the wand first along Sue and then Trevor. "You're fine. Go on in." He moved on to the next person.

Inside the tent doctors and nurses treated patients even as soldiers set up equipment, strung lights, and unloaded supplies.

A nurse asked, "What's your medical emergency?"

Sue stared at Trevor. "Well?"

"Ah … my daughter-in-law may have been exposed to radiation."

"What are the symptoms?" the nurse asked with pen poised on a notepad.

Trevor repeated what he had said to Sue, "Vomiting, fatigue, and dizziness. We were in Hillcrest, and within the EMP radius of the blast."

"That far south?" She shook her head. "That's the edge of the orange zone. We don't have any reports of fallout there."

Trevor felt his face warm. He had overreacted.

"Really, it's too soon to be showing symptoms." The nurse turned to a young civilian nearby. "Dr. Harper, can you take a quick look at these two? They evacuated from Hillcrest after the blast, but the woman is worried that she may be showing signs of radiation exposure."

"The man is worried," Sue said firmly. "I'm just pregnant."

"What are the symptoms?"

While Trevor repeated them, Dr. Harper had the soldier with the Geiger counter check them both again. Then Harper did a quick physical examination. He shook his head. "You've been through a lot, but I see no evidence of radiation exposure." He looked down the line of filling beds. "I've got to go."

Trevor and Sue walked from the tent.

At the edge of darkness, near the truck, a young man shouted and disappeared in the black.

"Thank you." Sue squeezed Trevor's hand. "I know you were just worried about me."

Still gazing toward his vehicle, he nodded. "I am worried." Then he recalled another person who would be desperately anxious, and his face warmed again. "Do you have your phone?"

"Yes."

"Could you call Sarah?"

She nodded, retrieved the phone from her purse, and turned it on.

Trevor unlocked the car, helped Sue in, and then walked to the other side. As he slid into the driver's seat, Sue held up her phone.

"There's no signal."

"Well, hopefully we'll be home soon." He started the truck, and slipped it into gear.

The vehicle shuddered, sputtered, and died.

Trevor stared at the dash, and then focused on the fuel gauge. The needle sat on empty. He cursed.

"What?" Sue asked.

"We don't have any gas." He threw open the door and jumped out.

"But you filled it." Confusion filled her voice. "I saw you."

He slammed the door. The locking gas cap, one of the few new devices he had added to the truck, remained in place. A glance at the truck bed revealed the gas can was missing. He thought for a moment, knelt, and gazed under the vehicle. All he saw was darkness. A hint of gas fumes hung in the air. He returned to the cab. "Hand me the flashlight in the glovebox."

"We can get more gas." Sue passed the light.

Trevor grunted as he shut the pickup door—slower this time. Buying gasoline had become increasingly difficult since the DC blast. He doubted he could find any now that Seattle had been destroyed. Dropping to his knees he shone the light under the vehicle and immediately spotted the problem. Fuel dripped to the ground like a clock ticking off seconds. He crawled underneath. Fumes hung in the air, and a small circle of wetness marked the spot directly below the drip. He directed the light on the underside of the tank as another drop of the precious liquid fell from a puncture hole. He recalled the young man who had shouted and ran into the night. That man had been the lookout while another had punctured the tank.

Angry at the thieves, himself, and the world, Trevor slid out, and stomped about looking for anyone filling a gas tank with his dented metal can, but found no one. Frustrated, he returned to the passenger side of the truck. "Someone poked a hole in the tank and drained it."

"You can fix it, right?" Sue asked hopefully.

"I can fix the puncture. Getting gas will be the hard thing." He stood there thinking for a moment. "Have you still got your pistol?"

She opened the baby bag and pulled it out.

"Keep the doors locked and use it if you need to."

"Ah ... what are you going to ...?"

"I'll be back in a bit." He walked along the busy road toward the dark gas station they had recently passed. The loss of the can would be a problem, but finding gas loomed as the bigger issue. The gas station that held out so little hope now held the only hope that lingered within him.

In the light of passing cars, Trevor counted a dozen vehicles at the station. Several, parked at odd angles, appeared to have been pushed to the station and then abandoned. A man cursed at one pump, begging the gas to flow. Shards from several broken windows of the store lay scattered on the ground. The shelves inside had been looted. A sign taped to a cracked window read, "No Gas!"

The owners would not have abandoned the station if it had fuel. Trevor walked away.

Near the military camp, a soldier filled the tank of a deuce-and-a-half truck from a tanker. From his army days, Trevor recalled that such trucks could run on many different fuels, even kerosene and heating oil, but he suspected the tanker held something more conventional.

Tents, sandbags and rolled barbed wire blocked off the fueling area. Perhaps a dozen civilians stood in a cluster near the gate. Several pleaded for fuel, but four guards with M4 carbines blocked their way. The soldiers stood tense, behind sandbags and barbed wire, weapons at the ready. One of the soldiers ordered a civilian to back away.

A middle-aged man shook an angry fist at the guards and cursed them.

Trevor moved on before the situation turned ugly, but his mind raced, searching for a solution. Near the medical tents, a tall colonel with light colored hair talked to a few soldiers.

"Colonel, could I speak with you please?" Trevor hurried toward the group.

A soldier, with rifle at port arms, moved to block his way.

"No, let him come."

The soldier stood aside.

"Thank you," Trevor said to both as he approached. He introduced himself and, without pause, continued. "Someone punctured my gas tank and stole all the fuel I had."

The colonel shook his head. "Unfortunately, that doesn't surprise me."

"I can fix the hole. Gum and duct tape might work temporarily, but I'll need gas. Not much, just a few gallons. I wouldn't ask just for me, but I have a pregnant daughter-in-law. I'm trying to get her to safety."

"Since you know my rank, I take it you were in the service."

"Yes, sir. Four years enlisted in the army."

The colonel nodded "I appreciate you asking and I empathize with your situation. We've shot several people today for trying to steal fuel." He sighed. "A hundred more have asked me for gas. Some have begged and pleaded. I've been offered money, Rolex watches, jewelry and more."

Trevor's face warmed, and he stared down at his feet.

"Most of the fuel we have is diesel, and I assume you need gasoline."

Trevor nodded.

"We can't spare any of it."

"Thank you for taking the time to listen." Trevor stepped away.

"However, we're transporting patients to the hospital in Olympia tomorrow morning."

Trevor returned his gaze to the officer.

"I can offer you and your daughter-in-law a ride with that convoy. That's the best I can do."

Trevor grinned. "Thank you, sir. That helps."

"The trucks will be leaving early." He pointed to the other side of the lot. "Be there, and ready to go, at dawn. Oh, and keep this offer to yourself."

Trevor thanked him again, and deep in thought continued to his truck. When he slid the key in the driver's side door, Sue thrust the barrel of the gun against the glass.

"It's just me." Trevor waved a hand.

"Give me some warning, Dad."

Trevor slipped into the driver's seat. "You rarely call me that."

"You're a great guy, but it's not easy to get close to you."

"No. I suppose it's not. Did you have any problems while I was gone?"

"No." She grinned. "But I'm glad you're back." She squeezed his hand and then they sat in silence for several moments. "I take it you didn't find any gas."

He shook his head. "No, but I did arrange transport to Olympia with a convoy tomorrow."

"That's out of our way, isn't it?"

He nodded. "I came this way to find you and Lisa."

"Oh? She's not with Sarah on the farm?"

He shook his head. "We've tried to call her, but no, we're not sure where she is."

"Of course we'll look for her. Why didn't you say so earlier?"

"She's always been in my thoughts, but we've been busy."

Sue laughed. "You are a man of understatement."

Trevor considered her words, and shook his head. They had been busy. How else should he have phrased it?

After a dinner from the gray lunchbox, and a trip to the latrine they returned to the truck.

"We may have a cold night ahead of us." Sue pointed over her shoulder. "Are there blankets in those duffle bags?"

"Yes, several." After retrieving them, Trevor tried to figure out how they both could sleep on the bench seat. "You lay down. I'll sleep sitting up."

"I'm not sure I can lie down on this seat." After several attempts she lay with her knees bent and head resting against Trevor's leg.

"Do you think Peter is alive?" Sue whispered.

Trevor took her hand. "All we can do is pray."

She nodded. "Dear God, keep him safe. Bring him back to me."

Many minutes passed before he heard the rhythmic breathing of her sleep. However, Trevor slept in disjointed bits, mixed with nightmares of death, cries for help from his children and agonizing, but fruitless, searches for them.

Day 2, February 8th.

He awoke, stiff, tired and sore, as the first truck pulled into position across the lot. Dampness covered both the inside and outside of the pickup windshield. He eased from the truck, softly shut the door, and went to find the colonel.

Trevor found him talking with another officer beside the growing line of trucks.

"I was just telling the lieutenant about you." The colonel motioned for Trevor to join them. "He'll be in charge of the convoy."

"Do you have gear you'll bring with you?" the lieutenant asked.

"I have a duffle bag and a couple of firearms."

"Hand the weapons to the soldiers as soon as you're on board." He pointed to a truck. "That will be the last vehicle. Get your daughter-in-law and your gear. I'll let them know you're coming."

Back at the pickup, Sue scowled at him. "Don't disappear without telling me. I'm worried enough as it is."

"Sorry." He grabbed the go-bag. "It's time to leave."

Sue slid from the passenger seat.

Trevor quickly packed as much of Peter's supplies as he could into his own bag, the baby bags and Sue's suitcase. They were overburdened for the hike ahead of them, but everything seemed valuable. He even put Peter's empty duffle bag in his own.

When he finished packing all that he could, he hid what remained under the seats and locked the truck. With a pat on the fender, he walked away hoping to someday return and retrieve it.

The lieutenant finished talking with the soldiers standing near the truck as Trevor approached. A medic jumped in the back, and helped Sue into the vehicle. Another medic offered to help Trevor.

"No, thanks." He grunted, and climbed aboard. Then he handed the weapons to the medic, and turned to thank the lieutenant, but he was already gone.

Trevor sat across from Sue at the back. Six cots hung from brackets on either side with patients in each. The medics set up IV bags and checked bandages as the convoy pulled away from the post.

Streetlights, cars, and homes should have cast their glow in Yelm, but no light shined. Nothing moved. Broken glass from cars and stores testified to looting and violence. Smoke drifted to Trevor's nostrils. It might have been from woodstoves heating homes, but he wondered if the fires of looters still smoldered. Only the growing light of dawn provided illumination and a sense of hope.

It didn't take long for the convoy to reach the outskirts of the Olympia metro area. The morning sunlight filtered through a smoky haze.

Sue turned to Trevor. "Where do you think Lisa is?"

"I'm hoping she's still at the university. That's one reason I accepted the offer to ride along to the hospital."

"Huh?" Sue leaned forward.

Trevor unfolded the wrinkled map. "The hospital is only a few miles from the school." He pointed to the two locations.

"Oh." Sue crossed her arms over her belly. "She has a car ... that old, two-door thing, doesn't she?"

"Yes." Trevor nodded. "If we find her, we may have a way home for all of us."

Sue glanced out the back of the truck. "But if she has a car and is okay ... ah ...." Her gaze drifted to the floor.

"I've thought about that too." Trevor bit his lip. "If she's okay and has a car why hasn't she already driven home?" He shrugged. "I'm praying that she's safe. Who knows? Maybe she's already at the farm."

Gray clouds greeted them as the convoy rumbled into the hospital parking lot.

After a heart attack scare a few years earlier, Trevor had spent a couple of days in the modern eleven-story hospital, but other than that had only visited there. Still, he remembered the many large cedar trees the builders had left dotting the area. What stood out as different were the military tents scattered on the lot and the large generators that thundered in his ears.

"Thank you!" Sue said to the medics as they helped her from the truck. She glanced at Trevor. "Gotta go." Then she hurried to a line of portable toilets at the edge of the lot.

Trevor turned to the soldiers. "Yeah, thanks for the ride." He shook their hands and collected his weapons. Then he followed Sue to the toilets. It might be awhile before they had the use of such facilities. Minutes later they walked away from the convoy and hospital.

"You said the university is close to here?"

Trevor pulled out the map once again and measured the distance with his fingers. He pointed along the street. "Maybe three miles that way."

"I can go that far." Sue strode ahead.

Trevor followed, staring at her feet. How far could a very pregnant woman travel in cheap tennis shoes? He shook his head, and prayed they would find Lisa. If they did, they might all be home on the farm for supper.

The business and residential streets they walked along were quiet, but not the peaceful quiet of morning before a busy day. This was the quiet of fear. Even as the sun rose higher, no children played in the parks and yards. Adults lurked in the shadows or peered out from cracks in curtains. Few cars moved along the streets.

With Sue a few steps in the lead, they crossed the parking lot of a burned-out strip mall. She turned to him. "Why would people destroy a grocery store?" She stared at the smoky remnants.

Trevor followed her gaze. *A combination of fear, desperation and greed.* Peter had dealt with such people every day. Hopefully he was still dealing with them. "In times like these hooligans feel free to come out from the dark corners of society."

As they neared the south end of the shops, three cars sped into the parking lot at the opposite end and screeched to a stop. Several young men jumped from the vehicles and hurried toward the smoldering main building.

"They look like trouble." Trevor grabbed Sue's arm.

"Yeah." Sue hurried along.

Shouts and curses erupted from behind them. Engines roared.

"You two, stop!" A gun fired.

Sue screamed.

"Were you hit? Are you okay?" Trevor hurried Sue around the corner.

She nodded. "Just scared."

They ran into the burned-out shell of a craft store. Light flowed in from the entrance, but the rear stood in deep shadow. Trevor led Sue to the back. "Hide in the stock room." He pointed and when Sue closed the charred door, he piled rubble in front of it. Then he hid behind a nearby counter. Smoke and fumes hung heavy in the air. He moved a few boards, creating an opening through which he rested his shotgun, watched, and waited.

Moments later, three men with pistols entered the burned-out shop.

Trevor sank lower and held his breath.

The first man, fat, with greasy hair, checked an open cash register. "One of them had a rifle."

"They're probably just passing through," the second thinner man said. "What do we care?"

The third man walked with a haughty air. "They didn't stop when I told them and we need more guns."

"What about the woman?"

He grinned. "I'll decide when I see her."

The porky guy laughed, and searched the far side of the store.

Stick-man searched along the near side of the shop. After several minutes he moved past the charred remains of art supplies, to frames only inches from where Trevor hid.

Silently Trevor aimed the shotgun.

Stick turned and shouted to his boss. "They're not here."

"I saw them run this way," Porky protested.

"If you were so near them, why didn't you stop them?" Stick ambled toward the front of the store.

"I wasn't that close."

The haughty leader huffed and shoved his fat cohort. "Well, since you think they're here, you can stay and keep watch."

"What? For how long?"

"Until we come and get you." He walked away, but over his shoulder instructed Porky. "If you see them, kill the guy and take his rifle. We need more weapons. But keep the girl."

Porky's mouth hung open, but he said nothing until the other two were gone. Then he erupted into a long profanity-laced soliloquy of hatred toward those who left him behind. He ended it with curses on his own life, and the world in general. Near the front of the store, he plopped down on a low counter and sat in cold silence.

Trevor barely breathed or moved.

Porky fidgeted, stood, ambled around the area for a minute, and then returned to the counter, sat and cursed the world. That routine continued sporadically for what seemed like forever to Trevor.

Trevor's legs throbbed from toes to thighs. His back hurt from the weight of the go-bag he wore. Even his neck ached. Staring at Porky he tried to send him a mental message. *Go check another store!* It didn't work. He wondered if he should just shoot the guy. Were the other gang members near enough to hear a shot? Would they come? He just didn't know and they couldn't outrun them. So, he waited.

An eternity later, Porky moved to the door and slid to the floor with his pistol on his lap.

Trevor struggled to remain still as his muscles throbbed in open revolt.

Minutes passed, but then he heard loud rhythmic breathing followed by soft snoring.

Trevor gripped the counter with one hand and stood on wobbly legs. Blood flowed into his tingling limbs. He doubted he could move, and prayed that Porky continued to sleep.

Gradually, Trevor shifted his weight and took a few small steps, all the while keeping an eye on his adversary. When his legs were ready, Trevor slipped the go-bag to the floor, slung the shotgun over his shoulder and pulled the pistol from his pocket. Keeping the pistol at the ready, he moved toward Porky like a lion approaching prey. Only inches away Trevor knelt, inhaled silently, and grabbed the pistol.

Porky's eyes snapped open and he cursed.

Trevor jumped to his feet and aimed both guns at the sleepy thug. "I need you to do some work for me."

"Huh?"

"On your feet." Keeping him at a distance, Trevor directed him toward the store room. "There's a door behind all that charred wood. Clear the way."

As Porky removed the rubble, Trevor called out. "Sue, are you okay?"

"Yes!" The door creaked. Boards moved. "Get me out of here!"

After another minute Trevor motioned with his pistol for Porky to back up. "Sue, I think you can push open the door now."

She did, and rushed to Trevor's side.

"A really young girlfriend you've got there gramps," Porky said with a smug grin.

Sue stared at him with angry eyes.

"I should kill you right now." Trevor's words were as cold as he could make them. He aimed down the barrel of the weapon at the man's head.

"There's a metal pole in the storeroom." Sue pointed. "Do you have rope?"

"I have a role of duct tape."

Trevor passed the pistol to Sue. "Kill him if he tries anything."

With wide eyes, she trained the gun on the thug.

Trevor wrapped the tape around the man, binding him tight against the pole.

"Are you just going to leave me here like this?" Porky's eyes were wide as he struggled against the tape. "I could die!"

Trevor added more tape to his legs. "I'd feel a lot more sympathetic if you hadn't planned to kill me, and kidnap and rape Sue." Trevor placed one last strip over his mouth. "If you work at it you'll free your mouth—eventually."

Porky's eyes flared with burning hate.

Sue pulled the suitcase behind her as they hurried away from Porky and the burnt craft store. "Will he be able to call for help soon?"

"Yes. Maybe too soon if he works at freeing his big mouth and not his arms and legs." Trevor looked about. "We need to hurry. Don't worry about him."

With one go-bag on his back and another in his hand Trevor struggled to maintain a jog. Sue followed, wobbled, and swayed as she kept pace along the residential street.

After a couple minutes of weaving along various roads, Trevor slowed, but determined to keep a close eye on Sue, he stayed alongside. Afraid the gang might hunt them down, he checked the area carefully. His shotgun rested on one shoulder, and the pistol stayed ready in his hand.

Sue stumbled to a walk and heaved giant breaths in and out. "I need to stop."

"Are you okay? Can you walk?"

She nodded. "Maybe."

Her pace slowed as the minutes slipped by, and Trevor found himself walking ahead of her a few steps. Repeatedly he slowed to stay near as they continued south along the two-lane surface streets.

Trevor heard the rumble of trucks before he saw them. When they crossed an overpass he gazed both ways along the interstate. A trickle of cars rolled away from Seattle, but most of the noise arose from military trucks headed north and tow trucks hauling abandoned vehicles away to clear lanes for traffic.

A block past the highway, the line of businesses on either side of the road yielded to an old growth cedar forest. Some of the trees, just inches to their left, towered a hundred feet into the sky.

Apartments and businesses catering to students lined the opposite side of the street. Trevor thought they were now in the suburb of Lacey. He increased his pace.

"Can we rest?"

Sue's voice came from behind. Trevor wanted to say no. In minutes he might find Lisa. They were less than a mile from the university. But when he looked back, the fatigue in Sue's face changed his mind. "Sure. Let me know when you're ready to go."

Sue stepped from the sidewalk to the nearest tree and slid to the ground.

He sat beside her and pulled a bottle from his pack. "Want a drink?"

She closed her eyes. "Not until we're at a bathroom."

While she rested he remained on alert. The breeze blew toward the highway, muffling the vehicle traffic. A car backfired in the distance, or was it gunfire? He tightened his grip on the pistol.

After several moments, Sue asked, "How close are we to the university?" Her eyes remained closed.

"This cedar forest is a natural area that belongs to the school. We're less than a mile from Lisa's dorm."

"Oh!" Her eyes popped opened, and she stood, using the tree. "I didn't realize we were so close." Sue pointed ahead. "That way?"

"Yes. Are you rested?"

She nodded. "Let's go."

Trevor stood and followed. He had driven to the campus only a couple of times. Because of the forest he recognized the area, but had few other specific points of reference. He worried that he might not be able to find Lisa's dorm.

As they walked, Trevor spotted a forest path. He looked to his right at a cluster of deserted fast food restaurants, pubs, and apartments. "This might be a shortcut to the campus."

Sue nodded, seeming to follow his logic.

Civilization faded as the ancient cedar forest embraced them.

The wheels of Sue's suitcase sank into the damp ground.

Trevor wanted to help, but with a duffle bag in one hand and a pistol in the other didn't see how he could.

Sighing, Sue carried it.

A hundred yards in, a deer scurried across the path and disappeared into the bushes. Trevor marveled that such a forest could exist within a modern metropolitan area.

"Do you know where you're going?" Sue asked from behind.

"Not really."

"Then are we lost?"

"No. We're still in town, and the campus must be near." He glanced over his shoulder. Concern etched Sue's face. He turned away grinning at the city girl afraid in a metropolitan forest.

When an ornate brick and wrought iron fence came into view, Trevor grew concerned. The gates to the school had always been wide open before, but now they might be closed and locked. Sue would never be able to climb over the twelve-foot barrier. He doubted that he could.

The path wound around a huge cedar tree and led directly to a C-shaped pedestrian gate, that looked something like one of the kissing gates he had back on the farm. Trevor slipped his pistol in a pocket as he entered the narrow twisted opening. He stood straight and held the sling of his shotgun so as not to bang the barrel on the wrought iron rods.

Sue followed. "This is embarrassing." She slid her belly along the bars.

Standing just inside, Trevor struggled to not stare.

"Freeze!" A man bellowed from behind.

Sue stopped, with eyes wide and mouth agape. Her belly still pressed against the metal. "Are you a guard?"

"We're just looking for my daughter." Trevor raised his hands hoping the man wasn't a hooligan. "She's a student here."

"The school is closed. You better go back the way you came."

Trevor turned slightly, but couldn't glimpse the man. "Can we at least check her dorm?"

For a moment no answer came. "What's her dorm and room number?"

"Cedar, 212."

"We've had problems with looters and vandals. Turn around slowly."

Trevor did as commanded and relaxed a bit. As tall as Trevor, the watchman looked much older, with a thin body and only a hint of gray hair left on his head. While he didn't pose a physical threat, he held a Taser and Trevor had little desire to see it fired at him or Sue.

The guard stared at both of them for a moment and then nodded. "Come on through, Lady. We'll check the dorm room." Then he locked eyes on Trevor. "But before we go, you need to put down that shotgun."

Trevor set it down. He still had his pistol in a pocket, and Porky's in the go-bag, but he hoped he wouldn't need to use them.

The guard motioned for him to move. "Keep following the path. It goes to the dorms."

Trevor stepped out quickly, but soon realized he had left the others behind. He looked over his shoulder. Sue held her belly as she marched forward. The guard kept a wary distance behind with Trevor's shotgun in his left hand and the Taser gripped in his right.

"Lisa!" Trevor shouted when he spotted her dorm. He broke into a run. Reaching the building, he yanked on the locked lobby doors. Frustrated, he waited for the others to catch up.

The guard arrived and slung Trevor's shotgun over one shoulder. Then he pulled a ring of keys from his pocket and unlocked the door.

Trevor hurried up the stairs and down the hall to Lisa's room. He banged on the door and tried the knob. It was locked. He banged again. "Lisa, are you in there?" Fear grew within him. Caden, Peter, and now Lisa … where were his children?

The guard shuffled down the hallway. Sue waddled behind.

"Okay," the guard huffed. "Don't break it down." Using the same ring of keys, he unlocked the room door.

Trevor stepped in, calling Lisa's name.

Sue followed, pushed by and went straight to the bathroom.

The space seemed smaller than Trevor remembered, and messier. Clothes littered the floor, covered both beds, and hung from open drawers. Blankets and sheets appeared to have been tossed aside. Trevor slumped into a chair. "Lisa, where are you?" he mumbled.

Sue joined them in the main room. "Peter always said that in police work he looked for the thing that was wrong or out of place. Lisa is neater than this." She walked around. "Much neater. I think she left in a hurry."

The guard lifted a framed picture from the desk. "Is this your family?" He handed it to Trevor.

"Yes, but not all of them." Trevor, Sarah, Sue, Peter and Lisa all stood in front of a Christmas tree, less than two months earlier. With the help of a tripod, timer, and quick footwork by Peter, everyone there was in the picture. "I have another son. He was in DC when …."

He couldn't bring himself to finish the sentence.

Sue turned the faucet, but nothing flowed. She pulled a bottle of water from the go-bag, drank deeply, and slumped into a chair.

"Sorry about your son," the guard mumbled. "Ah … you two can spend the night here if you like. The power often fails." He flipped a light switch and nothing happened. "Stock up on water when it runs." He shrugged. "I guess it's better than camping."

"Thank you, but …." Trevor glanced out the window at the sun low in the sky, and rubbed his chin. "Ah, our home is Hansen. Do you have a vehicle we could use or maybe some…."

The guard laughed. "There are several school cars and vans still on campus, but I can't loan them, and I've been ordered to conserve what little gas we have."

Trevor looked at Sue.

"Let's spend the night and start early tomorrow." Her eyes pleaded.

"Okay." He nodded. Several minutes later, after the guard left, Trevor searched outside the dorm for Lisa's car. Few private vehicles remained, and none belonged to his daughter. He returned to the dorm room and collapsed on one of the two beds. "If Lisa left here, where is she?" Silence filled the room. Suddenly, he sat up and looked about. "You left a note for Peter, perhaps she—."

"I've looked." Sue shook her head. "Sorry, Dad."

Trevor sat in growing darkness that matched his troubled thoughts. His mind lingered on family, but not the memories of joyful times past. Thoughts of death fought with despair. Had Caden died days ago in DC? Had his eldest son died yesterday in the attack on Seattle? Lisa? He had no idea what happened to her. And he had left his wife, Sarah, alone on the farm. His gut churned.

"There's some food in the mini-fridge. Not, much, but we could make a meal."

Trevor remained silent.

Sue walked to the counter. "I found two cans of spaghetti." She held them up. "I haven't had this stuff since I was a kid, but the only can opener is electric. Do you have mechanical one?"

Trevor pushed aside his worries. "What did you say?"

"Do you have a can opener?"

He reached into his pocket, retrieved a small silver device, and passed it to Sue.

She turned the thing over in her hand. "This is a can opener?"

Trevor smiled and nodded. "It's called a P-38, or a John Wayne. Not sure why." He took one of the cans and stared at the label. Did his daughter really eat this stuff? He opened them.

They sat on one of the beds while they ate the cold meal from the cans.

While they ate, the lights flickered, and then cast a low, dusky glow over the room. Trevor stared at a nearby lamp as the light grew gradually stronger. Water poured from the faucet in the bathroom and the toilet tank gurgled.

Sue grabbed several bottles from the go-bag and counter. "I'll fill these."

Trevor found a half loaf of bread and toasted two slices.

When Sue returned, she looked about. "Is there a radio?"

Trevor swallowed a mouthful of spaghetti. "I have one." He pulled it from his ruck sack.

Sue took it and slowly turned the dial until a voice poured out.

"… of refugees continue to flow south from the devastated Seattle metro area. Red Cross and military units are working to establish a ring … camps … walking wounded … unknown number of dead …." The signal faded away.

She turned the radio off and for several moments they sat in silence. "Peter will know to head for the farm, won't he?"

Trevor nodded. "And so will Lisa. They both might be waiting for us when we get there." He cast a confident grin, but his heart remained troubled.

A sad smile grew on Sue's face. "I hope so." When they finished eating, she pulled out her cell phone and tapped on the screen, listened, and repeated the process. "I can't get through to anyone."

Trevor walked to the window and stared. "We'll get home—to the farm I mean, and everyone will be there." Minutes later, the lights flickered and yielded to the black of night.

Behind him in the darkness, Sue sighed. "Perhaps we should make it an early night. We'll be walking a lot tomorrow."

He nodded, but sleep did not come easy.

Day 3, February 9th.

Trevor awoke to the smell of eggs and the sound of coffee perking. He stretched and stood.

"Did I wake you? Sorry, but the power and water are on. I'm charging the radio, working on breakfast, and topping off the water bottles."

"Breakfast?" He smiled.

"There were three eggs, and jam in the mini-fridge, and I used the last of the bread and coffee."

"Sounds great."

"Okay." She smiled. "I wondered if you had something better in one of the bags."

"Not really, and we should save the MREs for later."

She set the food before him as she scrunched her face. "What's an MRE?"

He grinned at his non-military, non-prepper, urban-born-and-raised daughter-in-law. "It's an acronym, Meals Ready to Eat."

"Oh." She shrugged and took a bite of egg. After they ate, she opened her suitcase on the bed.

Trevor bit his lip. "The next few days will be tough. We need to lighten our load. We'll take only what we can comfortably carry."

Sue's eyes widened.

"I'm going to repack our supplies into the two duffle bags. I'll need you to carry one."

Sue's mouth dropped. "Ahhhh."

"I'll make your bag as light as I can." Trevor sorted items from the go-bag on the other bed. He pulled an old pale green army jacket out. "That light jacket you have won't be enough. Wear this."

She frowned and put it on.

"Take socks and underwear and one change of clothing."

"One?"

"Yeah." Trevor nodded. "We might find a ride, but if not, we face a long walk home."

Sue wilted. "Okay, what else?"

Trevor tossed her a pair of hunting gloves. "Wear these and see if Lisa has a good pair of walking shoes or hiking boots."

Minutes later, Sue stood in front of a mirror wearing the army jacket, gloves and brown leather hiking boots. "I look like a homeless person." She wiped her eyes.

"When we leave here we *will* be homeless." Trevor walked up behind her. "You look like someone who will make it to the farm."

She nodded and sniffled.

Trevor returned to packing. He situated the majority of the items, and all the heaviest ones, in his bag. He helped strap the lighter sack on her. "How does it feel?"

"Okay, I guess. Let's get started."

Trevor hoisted the duffle bag onto his back and the shotgun over one shoulder.

A gray sky and haze greeted them as they exited the dormitory. As long as it didn't rain, or snow, Trevor preferred the cooler, overcast day for hiking. They left the campus through the same gate they'd entered, but Sue had to remove her pack to fit through.

They crossed the freeway using the same overpass they had walked the day before. No vehicles moved either way this morning, but thousands of refugees streamed south on foot. He didn't want to join the endless line.

"Where are we going?" Sue asked.

Trevor pointed. "That's Martin Way. It parallels the freeway and joins with other major roads south. I think it might be a good route for us."

From the side street they could often see the highway and later in the day they sometimes heard trucks and cars. A few times they glimpsed vehicles on or near the freeway, but none ventured on the road they traveled.

Out of habit they walked along the sidewalk, although the road remained empty. On either side only the burnt or looted shops remained. Windows were shattered; doors hung open or didn't hang at all. It was as if human locusts had plundered the land before them, leaving nothing behind.

Trevor kept a wary eye on the few people he noticed. Most hid in the shadows or moved away in a hurry. That pleased him. He had little desire for talk or another standoff with thugs like yesterday at the craft store.

They continued at the best pace Sue could muster, stopping only occasionally to check cars for gas or to rest. Trevor checked vehicles less as the day progressed, but time spent resting increased. Trevor told himself they stopped for Sue, but he felt the growing weariness of his legs and feet.

He knew the average person could walk about three to four miles per hour. Assuming a pace of twelve hours a day over flat terrain a person could do about forty miles in a day. He watched his daughter-in-law's slow shuffle. They weren't getting half that distance. If his math was correct, it would take eight days to reach home.

As the long shadows of evening stretched across the road, Trevor daydreamed of an open motel where he could take a warm bath, sleep in comfort, and call home to his worried wife.

Sue turned and pointed to a convenience store thirty yards ahead. "Can we stay there for the night?"

They were near the edge of town and he saw nothing but trees ahead. They would need to find shelter soon. "Let's check it out."

Glass crunched under their boots as they approached. Several cars sat abandoned near the pumps. One nozzle lay on the pavement. Another hung from a car. Trevor pushed the door to the side. It creaked as it slid out of the way. He entered and walked along empty aisles littered with crumpled packages, trash and shards of glass from nearby coolers. All food, water and other drinks were gone, either bought or looted. From the look of the store, Trevor guessed looted. Recalling his vision of a night in a motel, Trevor sighed. "Sure. We'll spend the night here."

Day 4, February 10ᵗʰ.

Had he done everything?

Trevor laid awake going over the events of the last few days. Clearly they should have driven straight home to the farm, and not stopped at the military post near Yelm. He cursed his decision, but he had been worried about Sue.

He gazed at her slumbering form.

Her gentle breathing told Trevor that sleep came quickly to Sue. For Trevor, that wasn't possible. He remained awake, listening to the sounds of the night. The breeze rustled through the trees. An animal ran across the pavement. An owl hooted.

He leaned against the wall as thoughts and regrets continued to flow. He had hoped that Peter and Caden would marry local girls and settle down nearby, but that hadn't happened. Caden left for the east coast almost the first possible moment. Peter stayed closer, but seemed to like city life. He'd met Sue while attending the University of Washington. They had married and settled in the suburbs of Seattle.

Sue possessed a strength that he had never before noticed. She had witnessed a nuclear blast, been shot at, perhaps lost her husband and, while very pregnant, walked and ran for miles. Well, the running was actually more of a slow jog.

He looked at his sleeping daughter-in-law once again. He would see her, and his unborn grandson, safely home or die trying.

Trevor turned his attention to the store and the preparations he had made for the night. The building kept the drizzle and dew off of them, but without power, no heat warmed the structure.

He moved shelves to block the door and broken windows along the front. Then they retreated to the rear corner, near the exit and an unbroken window. He located a broom, swept the area, and then laid out cardboard to insulate their sleeping bags from the concrete floor.

The temperature had dropped steadily after sunset, but he kept the sleeping bag open and loose so he could grab his pistol quickly.

As he listened for danger he placed his hand on the concrete floor. A sliver of glass cut his finger and he groaned. Despite his best sweeping efforts, bits of glass obviously remained.

He stepped from the bag into the moonlight and with his pocket knife dug at the injury to remove the shard.

Sue sat up. The loose sleeping bag fell to her waist. "I need to go." She rubbed her eyes.

Trevor pointed to the bathroom.

"That smelly disaster? It's clogged and overflowed on the floor."

He continued the hunt for the hidden sliver in his finger as he spoke. "Use the woods out back." His breath created small billowing clouds in the moonlight, obscuring his view of the cut.

"I can't do that."

"Bears do." He smiled at his own joke. "But, if you do go, I'm going with you."

"No, you won't."

"I'm not letting you out of my sight—well, I'll turn my back." He pulled the glass out and sucked on his finger.

She shook her head. "I'll wait."

"Okay, but don't leave without me." He took the broom and swept the floor around them again and then returned to his sleeping bag. He laid waiting for her to relent and tell him she would use the woods, but she didn't, and he drifted off to sleep.

Sometime later he awoke and rolled over. The moonlight now shone directly into their corner of the room.

Trevor looked at Sue's sleeping bag. It lay open and empty. He gritted his teeth, unzipped his bag, and stood.

A harsher light joined the rays of moonlight pouring through the front window.

The roar of an engine broke the stillness of the night.

Car doors slammed.

Heels clicked on pavement. "Why are we stopping?"

"We need gas. Get back in the car."

Trevor recognized the voice of the man—the haughty gang leader who had shot at them yesterday. Silently, he slid on his go-bag and grabbed his shotgun.

"How we gonna get gas?" the woman asked. "There's no power."

A glimpse out the window revealed Haughty with a flashlight standing by the cover to the underground tank, and a woman with arms folded across her chest in a nearby car.

"There's gas down here." Haughty pointed with his flashlight and then pulled out a cell phone. A moment later more curses filled the air. "No power and the phones aren't working!"

"The guys are coming," the woman yelled. "They'll be here in a sec. Just wait."

Trevor inched toward the rear door.

The light from a second car swept into the store.

Several car doors opened and shut.

Trevor knelt.

From outside additional voices arose.

"Hey, boss. What's up?"

Trevor recognized Stick's voice.

"I need gas." Haughty pointed. "There's some in the station's tank."

"I'll see if I can find some hose and a gas can," Stick said. "We should be able to siphon plenty."

Trevor shook his head. *You can't siphon from an underground tank to street level, but go ahead and stay busy with that while I leave.* He clutched the other sack, and collected the sleeping bags in a heap.

"Keep your eyes open." Mock concern filled Haughty's voice. "You don't want to end up duct taped to a pole like Manny."

Several laughed.

"I'll be careful," Stick replied.

Shadows at the front door caused Trevor to retreat toward the rear door.

As he drew near it opened.

Wide eyed, Sue stepped in. "I heard——."

Trevor clamped a hand on her mouth.

Sue stepped back.

"Shhhh." Trevor held up a finger to his lips and, with his other hand, pushed a sleeping bag into her arms, He spun her around, and together they hurried out the back.

As they crossed the parking lot Trevor detected movement. Gripping his pistol he glanced over his shoulder.

Stick watched them from the corner of the building.

Unsure of the thug's intentions, Trevor hurried into the woods.

"Boss, I found a hose." Stick called out. "I'll be there in a moment."

When Trevor and Sue were a hundred yards into the forest, and south of the station, they stopped and knelt low behind bushes.

Trevor repacked his sleeping bag. "Where did you go?" he asked in an angry whisper.

In an equally angry tone she said, "I had to, you know, go." She repacked her bag.

He leaned close. "Don't leave me like that."

"Why? You've been leaving me."

"What?" Trevor shook his head. "When?"

"When you discovered the gas had been stolen you left for nearly an hour. Then the next morning I wake up and you're gone, and why did we stop at that military station in the first place? I told you I wasn't sick. I'm pregnant!" She pointed to her belly.

Trevor stared at her. "Okay. You're right. I won't walk off again, but you can't disappear on me either."

"It's bad enough that I have to pee in the woods, but with my father-in-law standing nearby … that's not going to happen."

Trevor stood and pulled a compass from his pocket. "We can work on the details, but right now I think we should move farther away from the station."

Sue nodded. "Who was in the car?"

As he explained, Sue glanced in the direction of the station and then back to Trevor. "Okay. Which way do we go?"

"That might be a deer path." Trevor pointed ahead to where the bushes thinned.

"Huh?"

"It doesn't matter. Just follow and try to walk quietly until we're far from the station." With only the moon for illumination, they moved onward.

Trevor had developed the skill of trekking quietly for hunting, and now he prized it. He imagined that fear drove Sue to try hard, but pregnancy-induced waddle and wobble worked against her.

For nearly an hour they hiked up and away from the freeway. When they reached a tree-lined country road, Trevor stopped, listened and then darted across. Safely in the bushes on the other side he signaled for Sue to follow.

She did, holding her belly.

For the rest of the day they hiked deeper into the forest and away from the tattered remnants of civilization.

The sun arched across the sky. Shadows grew ever longer and Sue's pace slowed

Trevor knew they would need to stop again for the night. He stared along the narrow path, but saw only the deep shadows of the forest. Despite the darkness, thugs, and hungry animals, he felt confident that they would get home safely, but it would take days.

Day 5, February 11th through Day 7, February 13th.

Because the cool, westerly breeze and thick dark clouds threatened rain, Trevor had selected a campsite on a patch of level ground near the top of a ridge. The clouds held their moisture while Trevor erected the tent and the two retreated inside for the night. Exhausted, he easily fell asleep.

He awoke to the sound of pelting rain. Only the light of dawn illuminated the tent as Trevor slipped from his sleeping bag. The chill of winter sucked the warmth from him. Outside snowflakes fell to the ground and quickly melted. For the next few minutes the precipitation fluctuated between snow, sleet and rain. His spirit sank with each drop.

They had one day of food left, maybe two or three if they rationed, and probably five or six days of hiking. If they lost a day of progress due to the rain they would certainly run out of food. They must head south today, rain or not, but how far could they get?

Trevor sighed.

Sue stirred. "Is it morning?" She sat up and rubbed her eyes.

"Yes." He didn't know if he had either the energy or the will to hike in cold rain. "It's early though. Try to rest."

"Okay." She looked toward the tent opening. "Is that rain?"

"Sure is." He nodded. *The cold shower kind that seeps deep into your bones.* Trevor felt older, and more tired than his years.

"Ohhhh," she breathed a loud sigh and slumped to the ground.

Trevor let her rest for another hour.

"Sue, wake up." He touched her shoulder.

She swatted at his hand. "Let me rest."

"We should pack up and get started."

Sue sighed and rubbed her face. "I'm hungry. We should eat first."

"No." Trevor stared out at the muddy earth. "I'm hungry too, but we need to conserve food.

She scrunched her face. "I've got to eat for the baby."

"I'm telling you we need to ration the food we have." He continued to gaze out of the tent.

Sue lay down. "I'm not going anywhere if we don't eat something."

Trevor wanted to rest and eat, but he knew that would bring comfort only for the day. He stared at her limp form in the sleeping bag. "You're tired and eating for two. I get it. But if we don't keep moving, we'll run out of food and you'll be eating the rabbits and squirrels I kill."

Sue's face paled.

"Don't give up. We'll make it home." He leaned close. "I'm not dying here. I don't want my grandson to die here." He packed his gear. "I don't want you to die here. Don't give up."

She stared at him. "I'm hungry, cold and tired." Tears welled in her eyes. "Exhausted, actually. But, if you want us to go on today, I'll try."

Trevor nodded. "Good."

In the Northwest, rain could end in an hour, or go on for a week. He pulled the radio from his bag, turned it on, and inched the knob forward until he heard a station.

"FEMA has established camps in Olympia, outside of Longview and just east of Everett. Those in need of food, shelter or medical attention should report to one of those camps."

The announcer continued with emergency news, but nothing as mundane as the weather. He turned it off.

"I know we're not close to Everett." Sue pulled hair from her face. "Where is Longview? Should we go back to Olympia?"

"We'll get home long before reaching Longview and we're closer to home now than to Olympia."

Sue said nothing, then she sighed. "We should eat breakfast and walk as far as we can. Then we'll eat something for supper and camp. Skip lunch, not breakfast."

Trevor smiled. "Okay. Get a couple of MREs. I'll pack the rest of the gear."

They listened to the tap, tap, tap of raindrops on the tent as they ate.

When they had eaten, and packed their supplies, Trevor pointed to the top of the ridge just a few yards away. "This weaves south. We should follow it as long as we can."

As the sun rose, the clouds waned, and the shower eased into a drizzle.

The next two days blurred into a fog of damp drudgery as they hiked through the forest. The ridgeline Trevor had planned to follow dipped into a valley. They then trudged along a deer trail to a logging road that wound up a hillside. When they reached another ridgeline they followed it.

As usual for Pacific Northwest winters, rivers, creeks and streams flowed full and fast. Mud seemed everywhere. It clung to their shoes and pants.

Trevor's stomach grumbled. Every time they crossed a creek or stream Trevor wondered if he should fish. But it might be hours before he caught anything, hours that could have brought them closer to home.

His legs throbbed, his back ached and a blister on his right foot hurt with each step. On the afternoon of their third day hiking in the woods, the pair came to a clearing overlooking a river valley.

Trevor pointed. "That looks like a state highway, but I'm not sure what town that is." He pulled binoculars from his pocket. "Some of the buildings have burned." Columns of smoke rose from several structures. As he investigated each, it became clear that most of the smoke flowed from chimneys, but a few fires still smoldered. "I don't see any movement. No cars or people on the street." He shook his head. "The valley of the shadow of death."

"What?"

"Oh nothing. I think we should check out the town."

"Why?" Sue's eyes grew wide. "We've been making good progress and haven't been shot at these last few days."

"That granola bar you ate for breakfast was the last of our food.

"Really?" Sue's whole body slumped.

Trevor nodded. "And we would make better time along the road."

She shook her head. Fear etched her face. "I don't want to go into any city or town until Hansen. Hunt if you need to. I'll eat rabbits and squirrels—raw if I must. I don't want to get shot at again."

He stepped down the hill then turned back to her. "We haven't seen much game while we've hiked?"

"No, but—"

"If you want to, wait outside of town. I'll investigate and come back to you."

"Not a chance." Sue shook her head. "We're a team. We stay together."

As they walked down the slope, forest yielded to fields and pastures, but the two tried to stay out of sight using trees, bushes, and the gully of a creek.

Standing at the edge of a two-lane highway, Trevor looked toward the town. A dog barked and a rooster crowed, but he heard no other sounds.

Close to the town a sign announced they were entering Bucoda. Just beyond, a man tossed rubble from a fire-damaged convenience store. Other shops along the main road were either vacant, boarded up, looted, or guarded. A bearded man sat on a lawn chair by the entrance to a bar. Across his lap rested a double barrel shotgun.

"Don't stare," Trevor whispered. "Stay here." He walked to the man with the shotgun. "Hello, ah, we're just passing through—."

"If you want a drink leave your gun in the box." He pointed to a wooden chest beside him.

"No thanks, but where could we get some food."

He shook his head. "The church gave out food until a couple of days ago. People are keeping the little that's left."

"Thanks." Trevor rejoined Sue and the two continued down the street.

A man watched them from a used bookstore. A big "Closed," sign hung in the window.

A woman hurried along with an empty cloth bag.

As they neared the south end of the hamlet, it seemed the bar had been the only functioning business.

Children's laughter drifted from nearby.

Sue tilted her head to the side. "What could that be?"

Curiosity peaked caution in Trevor. The sound of something so ordinary now seemed extraordinary.

She pulled on Trevor's arm as she hurried ahead.

They continued around the corner where a grocery store dominated one side of the street. The building had been looted, every window broken, and the doors hung ajar.

In the parking lot, fires burned from four rusty oil drums. A dozen men and women stood beside them, warming their hands. Others lingered in small groups nearby, while children ran and played among them. Cars and vans formed a haphazard ring, something like the wagon trains of a different era. Five tents were pitched in a nearby grassy area.

Every eye followed them as Trevor and Sue walked toward the group. One man reached into his pocket. Another did the same.

Trevor forced a smile as he tried to appear harmless, even though he had a shotgun over his shoulder and a pistol in his pocket.

As they drew near, Sue stepped into the lead.

An older woman in a heavy wool coat stepped forward. She glanced at Sue's belly and with a gravelly, smoker's voice, asked, "Where are you two headed?"

Unsure of the group and not wanting to be too specific, Trevor hesitated.

"Hansen." Sue gestured toward Trevor. "My father-in-law has a farm there."

Trevor groaned inwardly.

Sue gestured toward the tents, vans and cars. "What is this group?"

"We're nothing but a bunch of forgotten refugees from the Seattle area." A tall, middle-aged man shook his head. "Forgotten and starving."

"Calm down, Ted." The gravelly-voiced woman snarled. "We don't want any more … well, just calm down." Then she turned back to Sue. "My name is Trudi. Most of us ran out of gas and hiked here like I'm supposing you did."

Several nodded as she said this.

Ted grunted and shook his head. "Others are so low on fuel they can't get anywhere."

"An army patrol came the day before we arrived." Trudi shrugged. "They promised to return with help, so when me, and my family got here, we thought it was a good idea to stay."

Sue looked at Trevor and then back at the group. "Would you mind if we spent the night here?"

One of the men smiled. "It's still a free country."

Trevor's gut churned. He felt certain several of the men had pistols in their pockets and, despite the women and children, he didn't trust them. People had posed their greatest danger.

Day 8, February 14th.

Awoman screamed.

In the darkness, Trevor yanked on the zipper of the sleeping bag. With his other hand he groped for a pistol.

Trevor found a gun and crawled to the entrance of the tent. The moonlight cast a soft glow over the area. Where had they camped? Then he noticed the looted grocery store and recalled that they had pitched their tent with other refugees at the edge of Bucoda.

Somewhere in the darkness the woman screamed again.

A shot boomed.

Sue stirred. "Did I hear—?"

"Someone is shooting. Stay low."

The burn barrels still glowed in the background, creating a silhouette of a woman running, followed by two men. Were they chasing her or following? Who had fired the weapon, and why? Trevor needed to know. He looked at Sue. "I'm going to the grocery store. I won't be long. Wait here." Then he stepped into the night, but stayed in the shadows as the runners entered the store.

Trudi's gravelly voice bellowed with curses. "Who killed him?"

Trevor followed at a distance. With light and quiet steps he entered the store through a broken window.

Angry voices drifted on the air, but Trevor couldn't understand the words. He stepped closer, but remained silent in the shadows.

Lanterns and flashlights lit a small area on the far side.

A woman wiped tears from her face.

Trudi stepped by a body on the floor. "I've seen him around." She looked at the tearful woman. "Do you know him?"

"Not really. He was nice though. He didn't deserve to die."

"Does anyone know him?" Trudi snarled.

Three men standing nearby shook their heads.

Trudi turned to Ted. "Why did you shoot him?"

"He stole from me."

She grabbed his collar and shook him. "What did he take that was worth killing for?"

"Food."

"If you're hiding food, I'll kill you myself. This family agreed to share things. Remember, we all survive or none of us survives."

Trevor eased toward the window he had used to enter. How many people in the camp were in this family? What would they do to protect one of their own?

Ted nodded and passed something to Trudi.

"Jerky? You killed him over a bag of jerky?" She shook her head and with an angry voice commanded, "You shot him; you dump the body in the river."

Trevor's stomach grumbled. He could understand anger over stealing food, but Ted had killed and Trudi planned a cover-up. He stepped back.

Cold steel pressed into his spine.

Trevor froze.

"Drop the gun. Hands up and move forward—slowly. "

Trevor did as commanded.

A moment later, the gunman shoved him into the light. "Keep walking."

With a face as rigid and cold as stone, Trudi stepped forward.

"Stop," the man behind Trevor commanded. "I found him listening over there in the dark. He had this."

One of the other men took the pistol and gave it to Trudi.

In the dark he had grabbed Porky's gun. His pistol and shotgun were back in the tent and of no use to him now. He prayed Sue would not come looking for him.

"I don't want any trouble," Trevor said with the gun still pressed against his him.

"Neither do I." Trudi marched close and locked eyes with Trevor. "But you were eavesdropping on a private conversation."

"I just heard shots, saw a woman run in here and thought I might be able to help."

"Going to protect the girl?" she smiled.

"Something like that."

"Very noble." She cast a sarcastic grin at Trevor. "We haven't seen any law since we arrived, and until now we haven't been harmed or hurt anyone." She glared at Ted as he dragged the body from the store. "We'll be leaving this morning. I suggest you do the same—and remain quiet."

"I'll do that." Did they have more gas than they let on? Could he retrieve Porky's gun? He wasn't about to ask.

As he hurried back toward the tent, Trevor expected to be shot in the back. But, if that didn't happen, what should he do? A murder had occurred. He should report it. How could he do that? Sue's phone hadn't worked since the blast.

Sue. She and her baby were his primary responsibility. If he wasn't shot, he needed to get her and his unborn grandson to safety. "God keep us all safe," he pleaded.

As he slid into their tent, he sighed with relief.

"What happened?" Sue stared at him with anxious eyes.

Trevor shook his head. "Don't ask, just pack. We're leaving."

Sue didn't move.

"Pack. Now!"

Trevor followed the state highway south but, to avoid detection, stayed just inside the tree line. Despite his best efforts to encourage her, Sue lagged behind. Still tense, he kept the shotgun on his shoulder and clutched the pistol in his pocket as he hurried south along the empty highway.

Soon the first hint of light appeared in the east. Frost covered the ground and billows of mist escaped with each breath.

Trevor shivered. Every bone seemed to grind against another. Muscles ached. He hoped the day would warm and relieve some of his pains. Sue had the advantage of youth, but the pregnancy, all the walking, and lack of food must have taken a huge toll on her.

He stopped and sat on a log. "I'm sorry about snapping at you this morning."

Sue faced him with hands on her hips and angry eyes.

"Remember Ted from yesterday? Well, he murdered someone. When they spotted me, I thought I might be the next to die. All I could think of is getting both of us out of there quickly."

Sue pursed her lips and her face softened. "Okay. I understand. Let's keep moving."

A yellow splotch on the gray-white clouds rose above the nearby hills.

For the next hour Sue led the way. Eventually, she looked over her shoulder and asked, "Do you know what today is?"

"Uh, Wednesday?"

Tears rolled down her cheeks. She shook her head.

Trevor hurried to catch up as he tried to think. Was it her birthday? No. It wasn't Peter's either. Then it struck him. "Valentine's Day."

She nodded. "Is Peter alive or am I a widow?" She rested both hands on her belly. "Does my baby have a father?"

Trevor swallowed. He had been so busy trying to survive that he hadn't given it much thought. Perhaps he had pushed it from his mind to avoid the worry that now washed over Sue. "He's alive. Until I know for sure that they aren't, I'm going to believe that all my children are alive."

He said the words with more conviction than he felt and finished with a smile. Secretly, he doubted that Caden lived and worried for Peter and Lisa. Fear churned within him.

By the time they reached the outskirts of Centerville, Sue's pace had slowed and she walked with a limp. She trudged ahead, but he knew she must be near the limit of her endurance.

"You have blisters, don't you?"

"I'll be okay."

Trevor knew they needed to rest. When he noticed a secluded area just out of view from the road, he said, "Let's stop. I'm tired."

"Okay." Sue followed him to the spot and slumped to the earth.

Trevor sat and took off his boots. Painfully, he peeled the sticky socks from his feet. Blisters had popped on each foot.

"How much farther do we have to go?"

"Today?" With his pocket knife, he punctured a blister.

She shook her head. "To get home."

"I think we'll get there the day after tomorrow." He stabbed two more blisters.

She lay like a dead person on the ground. "I'm so tired and hungry. I don't think I can hike another day."

"How are your feet? Take your boots off."

"Let me rest."

Trevor heard the babble of a creek. "I'm going to soak my feet and wash my socks." He grabbed a clean pair from the go-bag. "When I get back, I want to take a look at your feet."

Sue didn't respond.

"Do you have your pistol?"

Still prone on the ground, she reached into her pocket and held the gun up for him to see.

"Keep it with you. I'll be nearby."

Ten yards away, Trevor located the tiny brook. He moved a few rocks and scooped out sand creating a small pool. Then he inched his sore and tired feet into the cold waters.

At first his feet stung, but the pain eased. He sighed and relaxed. Tomorrow or the next day they would be home. He would take a warm bath and eat a huge burger. Finding a burger might be difficult, but he would devour a lot of something. Fried chicken? That thought made his mouth water.

A gunshot thundered through the forest.

Trevor grabbed his pistol and bolted toward Sue.

Seated upright, Sue held a pistol in one outstretched shaky hand. The other arm rested on her belly.

In front of her, a dark hairy form lay on the ground.

"Are you okay?"

She nodded without taking her eyes off the black and brown mass.

Trevor stepped beside her.

The hairy figure was a large dog.

"There were three of them at the edge of the clearing." She looked at him with terrified eyes. "They growled low and mean. I shot the closest one. The others ran off."

Trevor pulled a knife from his belt and knelt beside the dead animal.

"What're you doing?"

Trevor looked at her and smiled. "How do you like your steak?"

* * *

The next morning, Trevor awoke to the smell of cooked dog.

Sue hadn't watched last evening while he gutted and prepared the animal. She spent her time filtering water and refilling bottles. Would she eat the fragrant red meat?

She said nothing while they packed up meat for the next day, and buried the remains. Then they had moved a mile down the road to a new spot, away from the carcass, smells, and memories.

Then he had eaten.

For Sue, it took several hours for hunger to overtake revulsion.

Now, he heard movement outside and the rich aroma of the meat drifted on the air. Trevor's stomach growled. He unzipped his sleeping bag and sat up.

Sue's bag lay open and empty.

He crawled half out of the tent. The morning sun hid behind the trees and nearby hills.

"Oh, did I wake you?" Sue moved a small camp pan over a fire. "I'm hungry. I thought I'd get breakfast started."

"Take it slow, but eat all you need." He smiled, feeling better than he had in days. "Leave some for me, though."

They had both needed the day of rest. Trevor stood and stretched tight muscles. He looked up into a blue sky. Perhaps today they would make good progress toward home.

Then he joined Sue beside the fire, grabbed a well-done strip from the pan, and chewed on it. After eating the last of the dog, they packed up the camp.

Later they skirted Centerville, keeping out of sight within the forest edge. They climbed a small hill just south of town and Trevor used his binoculars to search for police, military or FEMA.

Along the freeway, the buildings and neighborhoods looked like a war zone of abandoned and burned out cars and smoldering rubble. Areas farther from the main road fared better, but he decided not to chance going into town.

As they continued south, blisters plagued Trevor's every step and, while Sue didn't complain, she limped.

From another hill, Trevor observed the hamlet of Maple. Closer to the freeway, little remained of the town's commercial center.

They paralleled the freeway staying up on the hills and in the trees as the sun moved from their left to its highest point that winter day.

Sue gulped mouthfuls of water from a plastic bottle as she walked. "Why do we keep running into bad people?" She passed the water to Trevor.

He took a long swig. "Most people have family or friends that help, and take them in during an emergency. Many bad people have ruined relationships with friends and family and can't obey the rules of the FEMA camps, so they end up out here, preying on people like us." He took another drink. "At least that would be my guess."

For the rest of the afternoon they hiked in silence. Birds sang from the trees, but they plodded along until the sun dropped below the trees. With the shadows lengthening, Trevor looked for a place to camp.

A large church dominated the exit just ahead. Several windows had been broken and four cars sat in the parking lot. As they drew closer a few more cars came into view along with the convenience store across the street. Still, nothing moved, except the breeze.

Sue pointed ahead. "This is the turn-off to Hansen, isn't it?"

Still watching for movement, Trevor nodded.

"We always drove right through without stopping, but when we got here I knew we'd soon arrive at your farm."

"Well, not so soon on foot." Trevor frowned. "Tomorrow, if we camp somewhere near for the night."

"Do we need to camp?" Sue shifted weight from side to side. "We could go on."

Desperately he wanted to get home, but his feet ached and Sue's limp had returned. "You're tired and your feet are sore; mine are too. Let's camp in the church. We'll start out early and be home for lunch."

Sue grinned. "Lunch, a warm bath and putting my feet up, what pleasant thoughts."

Trevor smiled and anticipated seeing his wife again. Would Peter be there? Would Lisa? He hoped so, but Caden … what happened to him? He would probably never know.

They entered the church through a backdoor. Trevor crept along the hallway expecting to find refugees. He opened every door and listened for voices or movement. People had been in the building. The halls smelled of sweat, the bathrooms smelled of sewage. Empty bottles, beer cans and food wrappers littered the floor, but he heard no one.

Trevor chose a Sunday school classroom halfway down the hall. If anyone else entered Trevor could hear, and have time to react.

He rolled out his sleeping bag near the door, slumped onto it, and closed his eyes.

"Ow." Sue grimaced as she pulled off her boot. "Darn it, that hurts."

In a nearby chair, Sue tugged on her sock like someone might slowly remove a Band-Aid.

As she did, Trevor spotted several blisters. "Wash your feet when you get them off."

"We're out of water."

Trevor groaned and, with muscles and feet protesting, stood. "I'll get some." He grabbed his shotgun.

"I'll come with you."

"No." He shook his head. "You're in no condition. I know there's a stream nearby. If I'm not back in twenty minutes, you can come hunt me down."

"Okay, twenty minutes." Sue smiled and held up her gun. "Don't be late."

He trudged from the room and out of the church. Several cars sat in the parking lot of the church and at the convenience store across the street.

Where are the owners? He hoped they had made it to friends, family or a FEMA camp.

Still wondering about the owners, Trevor reached the nearby woods. He had played near there as a child and recalled a small brook. Beyond the exit, the road sloped down into a small valley. The stream flowed along the bottom.

As Trevor filtered the water into his bottles, he heard voices.

Staying silent, and in the shadows, he hiked up a small hill that provided a good view of the highway. Still in the trees, Trevor scanned the area and then crawled onto a rock outcrop.

Logs and cars blocked the road. Five men with rifles, and wearing scruffy civilian clothes, loitered nearby.

What are you guys doing?

As he continued to observe, he realized they had established a crossfire kill zone. Four more men hid just off the pavement, in the gully right below him. In the fading light of evening, they were hard to see.

He surmised the hoodlums were waiting for a vehicle to come around the bend in the road. When that happened, the driver would spot the roadblock and slam on the brakes. Then the thugs behind the blockade would shoot, along with the men below him.

Nine guys, two angles of fire. Impressive and brutally effective.

He felt certain they would kill someone, but there was little he could do. Sue would come looking for him in a few minutes and he didn't want that. When he arrived home tomorrow, he would report it to Sheriff Hoover.

Trevor slid away from the edge.

The sound of engines bounced off the nearby hills. Headlights appeared.

He crawled forward. A dark SUV led a convoy of a Humvee and four trucks. In seconds they would be in the kill zone. Trevor eased the shotgun forward and pressed it against his shoulder. He had no chance of defeating the crooks, but a single blast from a shotgun might give the oncoming convoy a warning.

He pulled the trigger.

The boom echoed off of nearby hills.

Tires screeched. The lead vehicle of the convoy skidded to a stop.

More shots thundered in the valley.

The car reversed out of the curve as the Humvee behind it pulled across both lanes.

Soldiers fanned out as they returned fire on the bandits.

Trevor pushed back and, staying low, hurried into the woods. He planned to arc back toward the church and collect Sue. Before he reached the building, the shooting slowed and then stopped. He hoped the soldiers had beaten the men behind the blockade, but he had no time to find out. He needed to get back to Sue without being detected by any crooks. He crept along listening for movement.

"Halt! Hands up! Now!"

"Drop the gun," another voice ordered.

Trevor did as commanded. He figured they were soldiers; criminals would have just shot him.

As expected, two men in uniform appeared from behind nearby trees with guns aimed at him. One grabbed the shotgun from the ground and sniffed. "It's been fired recently."

The other man patted him down and then shoved him forward. "Move."

"I wasn't part of the blockade. I warned you guys by firing the shotgun."

"You warned us by shooting at us. Sure, I get it."

"Tell it to the major," the other said.

They marched Trevor down the hill to the convenience store across from the church.

An officer stood at the rear of an SUV. He pulled out several ammo boxes and reloaded magazines. "Are you guys okay?" he asked as they approached.

"Yes, sir. The shooters appear to have run off. The only one we captured is this old guy."

The officer turned toward them.

Trevor stared at the familiar but unexpected face. How could he be here? How could he be in uniform? Trevor struggled to form the word. "Son?"

"Dad?"

At the sound of his son's voice, he knew for certain it wasn't an illusion. Caden stood before him. Trevor fought back tears. "I've been worried about you ever since that first horrible day." He stepped forward with arms wide, and they embraced.

"I was worried about you too, Dad."

So many thoughts and emotions flowed through Trevor that it was difficult for a single one to emerge. "I thought…I, well…you're alive, thank God."

Caden stepped back. "What are you doing here? I expected you to be somewhere along the North Road. You didn't shoot at us, did you?"

"No! Well, not exactly." Trevor described going up the hill, seeing the barricade, and firing a warning shot. Then he asked, "When did you go back in the army?"

"I'll tell you all about it later, but right now I need more answers, like did you find Peter and Susan?"

"Not Peter." Trevor took a deep breath and sighed. "But I did find Sue. She's in a back room of the church."

"Let's get her. We need to get moving before the bandits decide to come back." Caden ordered the men to finish clearing the barricade, then regroup in the convenience store parking lot. "Keep an eye out for shooters and be ready to move when we come out of the church."

Trevor held out his hand, and a soldier passed the shotgun back to him.

As he walked with his son across the street and through the church parking lot, Trevor asked continuous questions. "How's your mom? Have you seen Lisa? Has there been any more looting?"

Caden answered each question. As they neared the church he clicked on his flashlight. "Do you think Peter was too close when they detonated the bomb?"

"I hate to think what might have happened to him. Sue and I were almost too near." He shook his head. "I can't see how Peter would have survived. I saw the flash and then Sue and I heard and felt it before seeing the mushroom cloud.

"My old truck was the only auto that still ran. It amazed me how many people were in the area. As we sped away, everyone ran in a panic toward us."

When Trevor finished speaking, they stood just outside the large church. The front doors hung ajar with one hinge broken and glass shattered. Caden pulled his pistol from the holster as he crossed the threshold. He flipped the light switch inside, but nothing happened.

By flashlight, the two men proceeded. Trash and debris littered the lobby floor.

"This way," Trevor whispered as he crept toward the hallway to his left.

"Are you sure no one is in here?" Caden asked softly.

"I checked earlier. We were going to spend the night in one of the rooms and then push on to Hansen in the morning."

"If it's deserted, why are we whispering?"

"I don't know." Trevor chuckled. "By the way, Sue is armed with a pistol."

"Oh? Does she know how to use it?"

Trevor nodded. "Yes. She does."

As they passed a lavatory the smell of human waste hung heavy in the air.

Reaching the middle of the dark hall, Trevor stopped. "Sue, it's me. I'm with Caden."

No sound came from the room.

Trevor looked up and down the corridor. It was the right room. He eased the handle down and inched the door open.

Sue stood against the far wall, old army coat on, and with the pistol aimed in Trevor's direction.

"Sue?" Trevor took a few cautious steps forward.

She exhaled and the pistol slid to her side. With her free hand she put one finger to her lips and whispered, "There are other people in the building."

Still in the doorway, Caden glanced up and down the hall.

Trevor froze in the middle of the room. "How did I miss them earlier?"

"They came in after all the shooting." Sue stuffed her gear into the backpack. "They ran down this hall, but I don't know where they are now."

"They must have circled back," Caden said. "They probably left supplies or something else important here."

"You don't have a radio on you, do you?" Trevor asked.

"No." Caden paused for a moment. "I'll lead the way out. Whoever is in here is either avoiding us or hoping to trap us. Either way, I don't want to encounter them, but if we do, I'll shoot. That should bring the soldiers."

"Why not just shoot now and alert them?" Trevor asked.

"I don't want to pull them away from the convoy unless it's necessary. We have three trucks full of food, ammo, and medicine, and a fueler out there." He took one more look down the hall, and then said, "You two stay low."

"That's a little hard to do right now," Sue said.

Trevor retrieved his go-bag and slid it on his back.

Caden looked both ways along the hall, and then crept from the room.

With Sue in the middle, the three crept toward the lobby.

At the end of the hallway, Caden leaned forward, his pistol ready.

A gunshot rang out, splintering the wood just above Caden's shoulder. He dropped to a knee and fired two rounds at a figure silhouetted by light from the convoy.

The man screamed and fell backwards.

Another blast and drywall flew into the air near Caden's head.

Trevor leaned forward and fired into the lobby.

Another shot, more muffled than the others, boomed.

At the corner, Caden glanced in the direction of the lobby.

The headlights of the convoy illuminated most of the area before them.

Caden shined his flashlight into the dark corners.

Trevor pointed to a body on the floor near the entrance.

The headlights blinked out.

Caden ducked back into the hall, and then peeked around the corner.

Sweeping their rifles back and forth, two soldiers burst into the lobby.

"Major Westmore here," Caden shouted. "Hold your fire." He stepped into the lobby.

Trevor and Sue followed.

"We heard shots," one soldier announced with wide eyes. "A man ran out waving a gun. We shot him and came looking for you."

"You did well." Caden looked about. "Check that end of the church. Dad, keep watch down the hall."

Trevor moved back the way he had come, as the other soldiers disappeared around the corner.

A woman screamed and ran from the sanctuary. "You killed him!"

Behind the screamer marched a second woman with huge hoop earrings and two small children.

The crying and cursing woman collapsed in sobs onto the body by the door. A young boy, with tears streaming down his face, stood beside her.

Trevor glanced back and forth from the sobbing woman to the hallway.

Sue edged back toward Trevor.

The woman cradled the head of the man in her arms as Caden stood silent watch over them.

After several minutes, the two soldiers returned. "We found one body on a pew in the sanctuary. I suspect he was the one wounded at the barricade. The rest of the building is empty."

Caden nodded. "We need to get the supplies to town. Let's get moving." He approached the two women. "You can come with us, but…."

"Look at all you've got," the screamer wailed. "Trucks that I bet are full of food, but we're starving. See him," she yanked the arm of the boy beside her, "my boy hasn't eaten in days."

While the woman continued to cry, shout, and curse, a soldier pulled back the sleeve of the dead man, exposing more of the tattoos on his arm. "These are gang related."

Caden stepped closer. "How do you know?"

"I'm a police officer in Seattle, or I was...."

"You were lucky to get out," another soldier said.

"Yeah, I guess. Well, anyway, I've seen these tattoos before. I suspect there are warrants out for the males. If they went to a FEMA camp, they would have been identified and arrested."

Caden stared in silence as the woman continued to cry, yell, and curse him.

Trevor watched anger mix with frustration and spread across his son's face.

Caden held up his hand. "Shut up woman, and—"

"No! I deserve to eat. And you know what? You deserve to die!" She yanked a pink pistol from inside her coat.

Trevor slammed the shotgun to his shoulder and pulled the trigger. Beside his ear, Sue fired her pistol. Bursts flew from the soldiers' rifles.

The crazed woman stumbled backward. Blood stained her face and clothes. She dropped the pink pistol and collapsed to the floor.

Earring woman screamed.

The children yelled. One ran from the room while the other hid behind the woman with hoop earrings.

Caden stood unharmed, but with wide eyes.

Sue let out a sigh and slid to the floor.

The pistol woman now lay across the body of the man she had once loved.

When the situation calmed, Caden spoke with the other woman, and encouraged her to go with them to Hansen. She refused.

Trevor recalled the conversation he had with Sue about why they encountered so many bad people along their journey. He watched as the woman walked away from Caden with her child in hand and disappeared down the dark hall. Was she in a family like those back in Bucoda? Had she destroyed relationships leaving her nowhere to go?

He would never know the answers to those questions, nor would he ever understand living in such a dark and desperate way.

Trevor watched as Caden picked up the pink pistol, emptied the rounds and slid it in a pocket. Then together with Sue he they walked to the SUV. As he did, it seemed a tremendous weight lifted from his shoulders. Those around him were friends, neighbors and his son.

They rode toward Hansen with the driver and Caden in the front seat. Trevor and Sue sat in the back, and conveyed the story of their trip as they went.

About fifteen minutes into the ride, the vehicle slowed.

Trevor turned his gaze forward. Ahead, lay the familiar causeway across the reservoir west of Hansen. On the far side stood a blockade of two bulldozers parked facing each other. Guards stood on the tracks and used the dozers as cover.

Sue gripped Trevor's arm.

"Don't worry." Trevor leaned close and smiled. "The guys on this barricade are there to keep trouble out of town."

The convoy stopped while one of the large earthmovers inched out of the way. Everyone exited the car, and Caden, along with the driver, approached the guards.

"We have three trucks of supplies and a fueler," Caden announced as he pointed to the vehicles.

"You got food in those trucks?" one of the men on the barricade asked.

"We sure do," the driver replied.

"Yes, we do." Caden raised his arm high. "Corporal, give an MRE to everyone on duty here tonight."

Shouts of approval filled the air.

"I'm going to take my family home." Caden gave orders to a sergeant regarding the supplies. "I'll be at the armory in the morning."

"Yes, sir."

The convoy and the SUV parted ways at Hops Road.

Through the trees, Trevor glimpsed his home several times before they rumbled up the long driveway to the farmhouse. His heart warmed when he spotted Lisa on the front porch. Another woman that he didn't recognize stood beside her.

Before Caden put the vehicle in park, Trevor stepped from the car.

"Mom," Lisa yelled. "Come here, you've got to see this!" Then she leapt from the porch into her father's arms.

Walking out of the front door, Sarah slapped a hand to her mouth and stumbled down the steps as she joined Lisa in hugging Trevor.

"I brought someone else." Trevor urged his family toward the car.

Caden stepped from the vehicle and opened the rear door.

Sue emerged from the car to more shouts and hugs.

As Trevor mixed with them, he noticed Caden step to the side and embrace the unidentified woman.

"That's Maria." Lisa grinned. "She's nice. You'll like her."

In groups of two, the family climbed the steps to the front porch.

Sarah turned to Trevor with a furrowed brow. "Did you see Peter? Is he okay?"

He shook his head as he pulled his wife close. "Moments after I found Sue, the blast went off in Seattle. We had to get away fast. We never had a chance to look for him."

Tears welled in his wife's eyes. Then she turned to Sue and rested a hand on her belly. "Is the baby all right?"

"The baby is fine, but I'm exhausted."

"Baby?" Caden asked.

"Yes." Sadness mixed with joy on Sue's face as she opened the old coat. "I'm pregnant."

Later, Trevor stood alone on the spot where, nine days earlier, he had worried about the future. Those days had been hard and he knew more hard times and sorrow were ahead, but he had brought Sue home. No. They had brought each other home.

These last few days had taught him some things. The greatest advantages his family possessed were their self-reliance, strength of character, and devotion to each other. He turned and watched through the living room window. Sarah brought a pillow for Sue's feet, while everyone talked and laughed. He nodded inwardly. This family would survive.

Also by the Author

Through Many Fires (Strengthen What Remains, Book 1) Terrorists smuggle a nuclear bomb into Washington D.C. and detonate it during the State of the Union Address. Army veteran and congressional staffer Caden Westmore is in nearby Bethesda and watches as a mushroom cloud grows over the capital. The next day, as he drives away from the still burning city, he learns that another city has been destroyed and then another. America is under siege. Panic ensues and society starts to unravel.

Final Duty (Novette) Twenty years after the death of her father during the Battle of Altair, Lieutenant Amy Palmer returns to the system as an officer aboard the reconnaissance ship Mirage. Almost immediately disaster strikes and Amy, along with the crew of the Mirage, must face the possibility of performing their final duties. Final Duty is one of a series of stories in this universe.

Titan Encounter Justin Garrett starts one morning as a respected businessman and ends the day a fugitive wanted by every power in the known universe. Fleeing with his 'sister' Mara and Naomi, a mysterious woman from Earth Empire, their only hope of refuge is with the Titans, genetically enhanced soldiers who rebelled, and murdered millions in the Titanomachy War. Hunted, even as they hunt for the Titans, the three companions slowly uncover the truth that will change the future and rewrite history.

About the Author

Hello and thank you for reading.

I grew up in the mountains of Colorado and went to Mesa State College in Grand Junction. When money for college ran low I enlisted in the United States Navy. I thought I would do four years and then use my veteran's benefits to go back to college.

While serving in the navy I wrote space opera and military science fiction. Both **Titan Encounter** and the **Final Duty** stories fall into that period.

My first assignment was with a U.S. Navy unit at the Royal Air Force base in Edzell, Scotland. Two years later, while on leave in Israel, I met Lorraine from Plymouth, Devon, England. We married the next year. Together we spent the remainder of my twenty year naval career traveling across the United States from Virginia to Hawaii and on to Guam, Japan and beyond.

After I retired from the military I taught in an Alaskan Eskimo village for several years while continuing to write. My first post-apocalyptic novel, **Through Many Fires**, became an instant hit, rocketing onto the Kindle Science Fiction Post-Apocalyptic list and eventually making it to the number one spot. The second book in the series, **A Time to Endure**, appeared on several genre bestseller lists and led to the recently released third book in the series, **Braving the Storms.** My books are available on all major online retailers.

Today, Lorraine and I live on a small farm in Western Washington State. You can learn more about me on my website: http://www.kylepratt.me

If you like what you've read

I am an independent writer, and so I don't have an advertising budget. If you have read one of my books and found it entertaining, please tell your friends. Also, the more favorable reviews a book has, the better it sells. So, if you liked the story, please consider writing a review on the site where you downloaded this ebook. If you don't like the story tell me why.

About the Newsletter

Once a month I send out an email newsletter about upcoming books, events, specials, giveaways, promotions and more—and I give a free ebook just for signing up! Use the link below. I respect your privacy and will never rent, sell, or give away your personal information.

Newsletter: http://kylepratt.me/contact/

www.ingramcontent.com/pod-product-compliance
Lightning Source LLC
Chambersburg PA
CBHW070505130626
46555CB00003B/1164